"People are like fabrics: some are silk,
some are flannel. You have to be careful
which ones you try to sew together."
—Hannah O'Dowd

To Anna, of course

DATNG

without

NOVOCAINE

Lisa Cach

**RED
DRESS
INK**
™

First edition March 2002

DATING WITHOUT NOVOCAINE

A Worldwide Library/Red Dress Ink novel

ISBN 0-373-25014-2

Visit Red Dress Ink at www.reddressink.com

Printed in Canada

ACKNOWLEDGMENTS

Special thanks to Anna Dudey and Scott Bodyfelt,
who provided invaluable information
on their professions.

To my extraordinary agent, Linda Kruger.

To my friends, whose experiences were
rich sources of inspiration.

And to all the poor saps who've gone out with me,
not knowing any better.

One

Sequins and Gossamer

Portland, Oregon

"Anoint your sacred body parts," Sapphire said, passing 'round a small blue-and-white Chinese bowl. "I made this rose water with the petals of flowers from my own garden, plucked under the full moon to call forth the power of the Goddess."

I slanted a look at Cassie, seated cross-legged next to me on a cushion on the wooden dance floor. She was wearing a short top that ended just below her breasts in a row of dangling, shimmering silver disks, her slightly poochy belly bare above the heavy belt of coins around her hips. She narrowed her tilted elf-green eyes at me in warning.

The bowl came to mc, the rose water a dark burgundy that smelled safe enough when I gave it a cautious sniff. I dunked my fingers in the water and dabbed the stuff on my throat and wrists like perfume, and passed the bowl on to Cassie.

With reverence, Cassie anointed her breasts and her

crotch, then bowed over the bowl and shut her eyes before passing it to the next novice belly dancer.

"I never knew you had sacred boobs," I whispered to Cassie as Sapphire invited the class members to share their experiences of the past week. "I would have paid them proper respect, if I had. Shouldn't you be wearing a more expensive bra, if you're carrying around holy orbs?"

"Hush!" Cassie scolded.

A long-haired woman with hurt-looking eyes started talking about the telepathic conversation she had had with her dog.

"You're going to have stains right over your nipples."

"Hannah, be quiet. You won't experience the Goddess if you don't open yourself to Her."

That didn't sound a particularly awful threat at the moment. The belly dance/goddess worship class of ten women was sitting in a circle around a small terra-cotta sculpture of figures linking arms around a lit votive candle. I'd seen the same piece in Robert Redford's Sundance catalog.

The psychic-dog woman finished, and a middle-aged woman with about fifty extra pounds showing between skirt and halter top started to weep. "My fiancé had to go to court this week. My neighbor says he flashed her, that he stood in our front yard and exposed himself to her. But he wasn't naked, and he didn't do it on purpose! He was wearing panties and gartered hose. He went out to get the paper, that was all."

Sapphire made soothing noises, while the other women murmured and cooed.

"If she's in touch with the Goddess, why is she dating a pervert?" I asked Cassie.

"Hannah!"

I shrugged. It seemed a reasonable question.

"It's time for the affirmation," Sapphire said, and everyone put their palms together in front of their chests, fingers pointing upward. Cassie hadn't told me there'd be an affirmation. I put my palms together and tried not to feel like I was praying.

"The Goddess has blessed us with wisdom and compassion," the women said in unison, touching their prayerful hands to forehead and heart. "She has taught us to nourish—" here the hands parted and everyone cupped her breasts "—and to create." The hands came back together and inverted, pressing down into bespangled crotches. Pervert-boyfriend woman parted her thighs to get her hands down in there.

I lifted my hands away. I didn't want to create with my loins, not while I was still single. Good God, that's what being on the pill for the past eleven years was all about. Didn't the Goddess know how to create with the mind or the heart? Or the hands? How about the hands? Leave the womb alone, for God's sake, at least until I got a husband.

And that, of course, was the whole point of my being here and subjecting myself to Cassie's belly dancing class of Goddess worshipers.

"If you get in touch with the Divine Feminine within you, men will sense it," she'd told me. "You'll loosen up the energies in your chakras, get them flowing. Men won't be able to take their eyes off your lower belly,

the center of your sexual power, and they'll be swarming all over you.''

Sounded good. I was twenty-nine, and it had been six
months since I'd had sex. Something had to be done.

I didn't know if warming up my chakras was going
to help things, but floating in the back of my mind was
a vision of myself in a gauzy costume, strings of tiny
bells wrapped around my hips, the faint shadow of my
pudenda visible through the fabric, nothing but heavy
jeweled chains concealing my breasts. Some strange,
thumping, wailing music would be playing in the background as I put on a private, belly-undulating show for
Mr. Right, working him into a froth of reproductive
urges.

Whatever Sapphire wanted to say about belly dancing
being about getting in touch with the Goddess and discovering one's inner self, I'd seen my Desmond Morris
on The Learning Channel. I knew that, anthropologically
speaking, this hip rocking was about showing a man I
was young and healthy enough to bear his children.

That was fine by me.

Once the nonsense about the Goddess was finished
and we started dancing, I started to enjoy myself. Sapphire demonstrated Snake Arms, Egyptian Walk, Lotus
Hands and an unnatural, rolling wave of belly muscles
that for some reason came to me with ease. There was
nothing attractive about it, but I knew it would come in
useful at parties when others were showing off their
ability to move ears or wrap ankles behind their heads.
''Sure, you can touch your eyebrows with your tongue,''
I'd say, ''but can you do this?'' And then I'd pull up
my shirt and give them an eyeful of rippling belly.

We stood in three staggered rows, facing a wall of mirrors and copying Sapphire's moves. My movements looked stiff compared to those of the others, my limbs about as loose and flowing as a senator's. I've always been one of those dancers who loses the beat and has no natural sense of rhythm. Maybe my sex chakra really was blocked.

We repeated the mantra at the end of the class, Sapphire gave us a homework assignment of watching for circularity in our daily lives, and then Cassie and I were out the door and headed to the car. Sapphire's house and dance studio were a few miles east of Portland, where suburbs give over to pockets of country, and we could hear a concert of frogs croaking in the spring night air.

"So what's with that blue rhinestone Sapphire had glued between her eyebrows?" I asked Cassie as we were driving home.

"I knew I shouldn't have brought you. You're going to make cracks about this for the next week and a half, aren't you?"

She knew me well. "And how about those little dots and diamonds beside her eyes? Suppose she used organic eyeliner to draw them? I mean, what are they supposed to signify? They make her look like a playing card."

"You don't have to come again."

"I don't think my chakra got any looser."

"It's not the only thing about you that's blocked," Cassie said, and turned on the radio so she wouldn't have to listen to me yak.

The dance lesson hadn't been a complete waste of

time. Watching pervert-boyfriend woman move with sensuous grace, I'd imagined her fat-folded belly transformed from a disfiguring burden into some sort of symbolic representation of Mother Earth, ample and giving. Despite the woman's lousy taste in men, the flowing way she moved showed she was in tune with herself in a way I decidedly was not.

I didn't want to admit that to Cassie, though—it went against the firm stand I had taken against New Age flakiness and vegetarianism. I also didn't want to tell her that while looking at myself in the mirror amid those other women, I'd realized I was neither as fat nor as tall as I'd thought I was. I was altogether smaller than in my own mind, and I didn't know if that said something good or bad about the inner me.

It occurred to me that I had been unfairly obnoxious about the class in my quest to not admit to kind of liking it. "Sorry, Cass," I said above the noise of the radio. I had been making fun of her religion, after all. "Want to stop at Safeway and pick up some Ben & Jerry's? I'll treat."

"Cherry Garcia?"

"And Chunky Monkey."

"Kewl."

That was the great thing about Cassie. She never held on to her pique, and any difficulty could be smoothed over and forgotten with a bit of ice cream. A girl could do worse in a housemate, and the Goddess knew I had.

I'd known Cassie since my first year of college, down in Eugene at the University of Oregon. Three years older than me, she'd already been at the school off and on for four years when we met. She'd joked she was on the five-year plan, then a year later, on the six. She finally abandoned all pretense of finishing her degree in sociology and turned her talents to her boyfriend's scented-candle business. She'd spend her Saturdays sitting in a stall at Eugene's open air market, candles arrayed around her, a book on how to awaken your intuition in her hand. To the right had been a booth selling incense, to the left one selling little pewter sculptures of dragons and wizards holding crystals.

When the boyfriend started dipping his wick in wax pots other than her own, Cassie moved up to Portland and went to work at Shannon's Pub as a bartender. She'd been working there ever since. Sometimes she sent away for brochures for career training programs, but they sat on the coffee table gathering dust and crumbs, until finally three or four months down the line, during one of our rare cleaning binges, I'd hold them up in question, she'd shrug, and they'd get tossed into the recycling bin.

She swung her hips to a wild and foreign drum, did Cassie, and I couldn't decide if I admired her for it, or wished she'd grow up and join the same concrete world as the rest of us.

Well, most of the rest of us. Sapphire and the woman who held psychic tête-à-têtes with her dog obviously lived in another realm entirely.

Later that night, as we sat on the futon eating ice cream and watching TV, a question slipped out that by all rights should have stayed tucked behind my lips. Maybe it was something about the dance class that had stirred it up. I don't know.

"Are you happy, Cass?" I asked, as on TV a woman with an ultra-white smile held up a tube of toothpaste.

Her slanted, lovely eyes glanced at me, the light from the television reflecting off them in the half dark of the living room. "Happy? What do you mean? Right now, at this moment?" She held her spoon motionless above her container of Cherry Garcia.

"Happy with your life, with how it's going. Is this where you expected you would be, when you became an adult?" I thought it came out sounding judgmental, as if I had decided already that she was not showing the proper drive and ambition of any self-respecting American. But the question wasn't truly directed at her, and she sensed it.

"Aren't you happy?" she asked me, and if there was a Goddess, she seemed to be looking at me with infinite compassion from Cassie's eyes.

I felt tears start in my own, taking me by surprise, and I tightened my lips against the sudden quivering there.

"Oh, sweetie," Cassie said as the *X-Files* theme started whistling in the background. "It'll be all right. You expect too much of yourself, is all."

"But..." I blubbered, a vast blackness of want seeping up from the dark depths, the ice cream in my hand a cold and empty comfort. "But there's so much I—"

"So much you thought you'd have by now? Husband, children, SUV, golden retriever? A house in the west hills?"

"A Volvo, not an SUV—"

"Hannah, you're so predictable," Cassie said, and somehow her gently sardonic tone was comforting.

"Everyone thinks they're supposed to want those things, but I don't think you really do."

"Yes I do. Especially the husband."

"If you were ready, you'd have one. Maybe right now you're doing exactly what you're supposed to be doing."

I looked down at my Chunky Monkey. "You think so?"

"It's your sewing business that matters to you. That's why you moved up to Portland to begin with. Concentrate on that, and let the universe handle the rest in its own time."

I wished I had her faith that all would come right in the end. It seemed to come so easily to her, so naturally. I never saw Cassie worry about anything. "Can't I have a little of the rest right now? Like a boyfriend?" I asked.

"He'll come when you're ready." She smiled. "In the meantime, there's David Duchovny."

I looked at the screen, where Mulder and Scully were arguing in a repeat episode, and sniffed back the remainder of my weepy self-pity. "I don't want him."

"Why not? I'd do him."

"He never smiles," I said.

"You don't want a guy to be grinning while he's got your legs over his shoulders. Talk about creepy." She shuddered, and I gave a small laugh, glad of the change of topic and of mood.

"Can't be much worse than how they usually look." I squeezed my eyes shut and groaned as though I was in pain, straining out the words, "I'm coming, I'm coming! I'm almost there... Can I come? Can I come now?"

"They ask you that?"

"One of my ex-boyfriends used to."

"Did you let him?" Cassie asked.

"Depends how long he'd been going at it. Past a certain point, I just wanted him to get it over with. I started thinking about urinary tract infections."

Cassie winced, and I knew both our minds had gone to the unopened jug of cranberry juice in the cupboard, kept there in case of emergency.

"Maybe it's for the best that your sex chakra is blocked up," Cassie said.

"Maybe you're right."

Two

Orange Tiers with Bric-a-brac Trim

Tuesday evening found me knee-deep in bridesmaids' dresses, my Bernina sewing machine humming smoothly up and down seams and around armholes. I'm a seamstress, and have my own pick-up-and-deliver alterations and custom sewing business, Hannah's Custom Sewing. I'd left off my last name, O'Dowd, as it had less than desirable connotations for one whose work was mainly with clothing.

Six months ago I had been living in Eugene, working in an alterations shop. My degree in history was going as unused as Cassie's coursework in sociology, but I didn't care. I'd realized that the only part of history that I really liked was examining the clothes in old paintings. The French Revolution was more interesting to me for its effect on fashion than for its effect on the French aristocracy, although the two were inextricably intertwined. Any history paper where I'd had the choice of topic had focused, in some manner or another, on clothing.

When my off-and-on boyfriend of two years had at last been permanently switched off, I'd taken a page

from the Book of Cassie and decided to move up to
Portland. I was tired of Eugene with its determined tofu-
eating and tie-dye, and tired, as well, of working for
someone else. The alterations shop had been turning
away business, there was so much of it, and I felt certain
I'd be able to find ample work for myself up in Portland,
where people actually bothered to wear clothes that fit.
To make my services special, I would pick up and deliver clothes and other sewing work to people's homes
and businesses. That would also save me from worrying
that someone would slip and fall on my front steps and
decide to sue me.

It's a good thing I like to drive. I've put nearly ten
thousand miles on my Neon since I've been in Portland.

The first few months I barely managed to scrape by,
and used up all my savings staying ahead of car pay-
ments, gas, insurance, and that nagging little lump of
credit card debt that festered like a nasty pimple, never
completely going away. These last two months, though,
I had hit some sort of critical sewing mass, and I had a
steady stream of clients, some of whom had already become regulars. I made more money than I had at the
alterations shop, but on my own I didn't have health
insurance or paid sick days. I was debating which to
buy first—the health insurance or a hemmer.

My sewing room is upstairs in the small 1920's stucco
house that Cassie and I share. In exchange for taking up
two rooms to her one, every four or five weeks I make
her a new dance costume or something for her room,
like a new comforter cover or floor pillows. This month
was going to be curtains, made out of some filmy Middle Eastern material she'd bought at a belly dancing fes-

tival. I think I'll put bells on the bottom, just for the fun of it. When the wind moves the curtains, they'll make soft tinkling sounds. Cassie will like that.

I glanced at the clock and grimaced: 7:00 p.m. I was due at San Juan's Mexican Restaurant in half an hour. Cassie, Louise, Scott and I were all meeting for dinner, to celebrate Louise finally getting off nights and onto days at the crisis line. She'd been working there for two years, and the screwy sleeping schedule and proscribed social life had driven her to the brink of clinical depression. And she should know, being a counselor and dealing with the mentally ill all night.

I slipped the jacket I was working on onto a hanger and hung it up along with the others, giving the lineup a critical look. The bride, genuinely concerned that her bridesmaids be able to wear their clothes again, and having the good taste to abhor butt bows, taffeta and sleeve less dresses that exposed flabby upper arms, had chosen to garb her friends in Jackie O-style skirt suits in a neutral blue.

It was a nice idea, but all lined up together I feared the bridesmaids might look like 1960's flight attendants. All they needed was a pair of wings pinned to their lapels and pillbox hats, and the guests would be expecting them to throw peanut packets instead of flower petals as they walked down the aisle.

I shrugged. It wasn't my problem. I'd learned long ago to let clients decide for themselves what they wanted. There was too wide a range of tastes out there for me to try to advise anyone, based on my own limited preferences.

My pants were creased from sitting, blue threads and

fabric fuzz stuck to them like paint on a Jackson Pollock. I stripped the pants off and pulled on a short tailored skirt of gray faille. I had sixteen skirts of the exact same cut, made from fabric remnants from various jobs. On top I wore a short-sleeved light blue cashmere crewneck, found for twenty-four dollars at Nordstrom Rack. I'd repaired the hole in the armpit that had relegated the treasure to the bargain pile. It brought out the blue in my blue-gray eyes, and was my favorite piece of clothing.

I put in small crystal studs and gave my chin-length bob a quick brushing. The color was presently a soft honey-blond, darker than the over-highlighted tresses I'd worn in Eugene. When the boyfriend had gone, so had my long hair. I'd sat myself down at the salon and told the stylist to give me hair that would attract professional men with marriage on their minds, instead of the usual unemployed gorillas who came on to me. I've never understood why it is that the men with the least to offer are the ones the most willing to make a pass at a woman.

My new hair hadn't given me any success with the eligible men yet, but at least the shiftless ones had left me alone. Louise said it was the new, determined look in my eyes that scared the losers away, not the hair. I hoped that wasn't the explanation for the lack of professional men, as well.

Scott and Louise were waiting in the foyer of the restaurant when I arrived, sitting on a bench eating chips. The peasant-bloused staff gave out baskets of them when the wait for a table was over ten minutes, which was one reason the place was a favorite of ours.

"Hannah!" Louise said, scooting over to make space for me on the bench. "Where's Cassie?"

"I don't know. She'll be here. Hi, Scott."

"Hi," he said, smiling his usual friendly smile. He and Louise had been boyfriend and girlfriend senior year in high school, and he'd been Louise's "first" in both love and sex. The relationship hadn't lasted over a year into college—Scott had gone to Cornell, Louise to Oregon—but they'd remained friends, and Scott had become friends with Cassie and me, as well, when each of us in turn had moved up to Portland.

It was silently understood that Louise, while willing to share Scott as a friend, would not look kindly upon either Cassie or me taking him on as anything more. I couldn't blame her—the thought of my first love sleeping with either Cassie or Louise set my teeth on edge.

With that past relationship serving as a symbolic sword on the bed between us, I'd found that I was more comfortable with Scott than with men who were available. He was tall and reasonably good-looking, with dark hair and a slightly boyish face with a dimple in his chin. I occasionally helped him shop for clothes, and when the weather was nice we'd sometimes go for a hike together.

"Hey, Scott, I've got a new one for you," I said, leaning forward to see him around Louise.

He groaned. "Your jokes are never new. I've heard them all a hundred times."

"This one's a limerick."

"Please, no."

"I want to hear it," Louise said, brown eyes sparkling

in her freckled face. She enjoyed teasing Scott about his
profession nearly as much as I did.

"Okay, here goes.

> 'There was a young dentist Malone
> Who had a charming girl patient alone
> But in his depravity
> He filled the wrong cavity
> My, how his practice has grown!' "

Louise laughed, but Scott put his hands over his face
and shook his head. "That one's older than George
Washington's dentures," he complained. "I have to listen to this type of lame humor all day at work. Why do
you have to inflict it on me after hours?"

"Because dentists deserve punishment. They're evil
people."

Louise put her hand on my knee and gave me her
mock therapist look. "I'm sensing a deep childhood
trauma, Hannah. You're safe here. You can talk about
it."

"The memories, I only see flashes of them, a man in
a white coat, the whine of a drill—no! No!"

Louise turned to Scott. "She's repressed the memories. We'll have to try hypnosis. This woman has been
deeply scarred. Your presence obviously brings up pain-
ful feelings for her."

Scott was about to respond when Cassie swept in,
bringing a wave of patchouli and sandalwood with her
that temporarily overwhelmed the chili pepper odors of
the restaurant. "Sorry I'm late! Practice ran later than
expected." Cassie belonged to a semi-professional belly

dance troupe, and her first public performance was coming up in a few weeks.

Louise waved her hand in a gesture to say it didn't matter. "Our table isn't ready yet anyway."

The teenage hostess called Louise's name just then, and we followed her swaying, tiered gathers of orange skirt with pink bric-a-brac into the dining area, Scott and me falling behind Cassie and Louise.

"Did I tell you about the Japanese exchange student I saw last week, the one who hadn't been to a dentist in over ten years?" Scott asked. "One of his molars had cracked, and the nerve was exposed. I had to—"

"Stop it! Stop it!" I cried, putting my hands over my ears. Hearing about dental disasters was even worse to me than listening to stories about someone getting their eye poked out. This, however, was Scott's usual revenge for my dentist jokes: his most revolting cases recounted in excruciating detail for my torture. I don't think he knew how very real my fear of dentists was, under all the joking.

And it wasn't that anything truly horrible had ever happened while I was under the gas and drill: no wrong tooth accidentally removed, no hygienist slipping with her little metal scraper and gouging my gums, no near-choking experience with those tooth trays of drool-producing fluoride I got as a kid.

It was instead a lifetime's worth of anxious dread, of the taste of topical anaesthetic before the needleful of novocaine went in, of spitting out small chunks of tooth after the drilling was finished and the filling put in.

I hated going to the dentist, I hated dentists on general principle, and since I had no insurance I was enjoying the relatively guilt-free thought that I couldn't afford to go to one for quite a long while.

We gave our orders and settled down to a fresh basket of chips, two types of salsa and kidney-straining quantities of diet soda. Except, that is, for Scott, who rode his bike about forty miles every other day and didn't have to worry about the dimensions of his derriere. He eschewed diet soda for a Dos Equis.

"I can't believe I'm going to have a normal life," Louise said, her straw making loud suction sounds at the bottom of her ice-filled glass. Scott flagged down a passing busboy, who took away Louise's empty glass for replacement. "My life will no longer revolve around sleep! I can go out in the evenings, I can see the sun on weekends. I've already taken the blankets down off my windows."

"You're like a plant, ready to grow," Cassie said. "You've been in the dark too long, getting yellow."

"Exactly!" Louise said. She held out her pale, freckled forearm for us all to see. "This is not the color of a healthy human being."

"Now you won't have an excuse not to start dating," I said.

Louise made a duck face with her lips, her eyes narrowing. "I'm sure I could think of one."

"How long has it been since you broke up with that guy who worked at Intel?" I asked.

"I wouldn't call it 'breaking up.' We only went out a few times. That doesn't constitute a relationship."

"But how long ago was it?" I persisted.

"Three months, give or take, and I'm in no hurry to repeat the experience. I just don't do well with technical men—I think it's a basic personality conflict. They're all Sensing-Thinking types, and I'm an Intuitive-Feeler, like Cass. But of course the only available guys work in computers. Why is that?''

''It's a major industry in the region,'' Scott said, ''so of course there are lots of guys around who work in computers.'' We all gave him dirty looks. Sometimes he failed to catch the true substance of a discussion.

''No, I think it's because they're the only ones left who are single,'' Louise said. ''And there's a reason for that, in terms of their emotional development—or lack thereof. They're all geeks, who've put all their efforts to learning about things instead of people.''

''Geeks have their advantages,'' I said. ''They usually have good jobs, and they treat you well, they're so glad to have you.''

''Have you ever dated one?'' Scott asked.

''Well, no.''

''I didn't think so. They don't seem to be your type,'' he said.

''What *is* my type?''

''I don't know. Someone edgier.'' He widened his eyes. ''Dangerous.''

I snickered. ''Yeah, right. The muscle-bound sort, with long hair and tattoos. Motorcyclists who ride without helmets. Bad boys, the type who group together to rent a house in northeast Portland and wouldn't know a lawn mower if it ran over their foot. Probably don't vote, either. That's the type for me!''

''Hannah, dear,'' Louise said, ''I don't know a single woman who finds a man who avoids yardwork attractive.''

"And long hair is only nice in fantasies," I said. "In real life, it's the sign of a guy who has to sell his motorcycle to find money for this month's rent."

"I like guys with long hair," Cassie said. "They don't have to be losers—I know several emotionally aware ones in my yoga class, one of whom teaches English at Portland State. I think long hair's sexy."

I looked at Scott, trying to imagine him with long hair, the heavy mass of it pulled back in a ponytail while he walked around his office in blue-green scrubs. It wasn't an entirely unpleasant picture, but it was pretty funny.

He caught me looking at him, and saw the smirk on my face. "What?" he asked.

"Nothing."

Our food came, platters of fajita fillings sizzling and steaming in dramatic fashion. For a few minutes all thoughts were turned to tortillas and sour cream, as we filled and rolled. With my first bite I felt fajita juice drip out the bottom and run over my hand.

"I don't know why I should be the only one pestered to start dating," Louise said after we'd all downed the first crucial mouthfuls. "Not a one of you is doing so yourself. You're projecting onto me."

"I'm trying to date," I said. "God knows I'm trying. I just can't seem to find anyone suitable."

"Her sex chakra is blocked up," Cassie said.

"What?" Scott asked, his pristine, undripping fajita halted halfway to his mouth.

"My sex chakra," I said, and leaning back pointed to the area just below my navel. "Cass was trying to help me free my sexual energy by taking me to a belly dance class.''

"Men can sense when the Divine Feminine has been awakened in a woman," Cassie said.

"They can?" Scott asked.

"Maybe that's what I need to do," Louise said, to no one in particular.

"If you're not seeing anyone," Cassie said to Scott, "your own sex chakra might have a blockage."

"I'm not going to try belly dancing," he said.

"I don't know the proper moves for men, anyway," Cassie said. "The energies are different. Drinking a lot of fluids is supposed to help, though, for both men and women. It flushes you out."

Apparently water was not only good for conventional constipation, but emotional, as well. I refrained from making note of it out loud, considering we were eating. I saw Scott's lips twitch. Our eyes met briefly, and I knew he was thinking the same thing.

"Where are we supposed to meet people these days, anyway?" Louise asked. "I don't want to go to a bar, much less date someone who hangs out in one looking for women. Going through parents or friends is supposed to be what all the 'experts' advise, but my parents don't know anyone of the right age—I've asked. All they can come up with is someone's twenty-five-year-old, ultra-Christian son. And you all are no help. If you did find a single guy, you'd go for him yourselves."

"I wouldn't," Scott said.

"You were supposed to find me a nice dentist. Where is he?" Louise asked.

"They're all married," he said. "And besides, they're

not your type. You need someone who'd be willing to talk all night about Jungian dream analysis, not some guy who'd rather be out boating on the river, cruising by Sauvie's Island to spy on the nude sunbathers.''

"Is that what dentists do on their days off?" I asked.

"Only when they're not polishing their Porsches or hanging out at The Sharper Image.''

We were quiet for a moment, each of us stewing over the perpetual adolescence of men, while Scott wrapped up another fajita.

"This really can't be as hopeless as it all seems," I finally said. "Even if there is only one man in a million who would be right for each of us, there's what, two million people in the greater Portland area? So one million men, which means one guy who would be perfect. For each of us. And one woman for you, Scott. They're out there—we just have to find them."

"You can't force these things," Cassie said. "The universe—"

"I don't want to wait for the universe to take care of it. I'm going to be thirty years old on September sixth— that's four months away. I want to be engaged by then," I said, resolved on the issue, all my angst of the other night suddenly crystallizing on this one point. It was as if making a declaration would take away all the uncertainty, all the worry about what my future would be. Nothing had changed, but it gave me a sense of control, however spurious. "I don't want to turn thirty and still not know who I'm going to marry."

"Hannah," Louise said in a concerned, counselor tone, "getting married just because you think you're the age that you should is setting yourself up for disaster."

"Well, I'm not going to just grab some poor fool off the street. If I was willing to marry *anyone* there wouldn't be a problem. No, I'm going to find Mr. Right—the one-in-a-million Mr. Right who is within a twenty-mile radius of us as we speak. Then it won't be a mistake at all."

"Why the big concern about turning thirty?" Scott asked.

We all looked at him. Again, his maleness was showing.

"I mean, I had a big bash when I turned thirty. It was great—you know, you were there. Yeah, I felt a little old, but I certainly wasn't worried about getting married."

"Tick, tick, tick," I said.

He looked blank.

"The biological clock," I said. "It's ticking. You can have kids until the Viagra gives out, but we've got deadlines to meet."

"Women are having children well into their forties—"

"I don't think any of us wants to be eligible for social security when our kids graduate from high school," I said. "I don't want to worry that my husband is going to die of a heart attack while playing basketball with my son. I don't want people to assume I'm my daughter's grandmother. I've got an independent career, I make my own hours and my own money, now I want a husband and to start a family. It's time, whether the universe thinks so or not, and I'm going to do something about it."

"Jeez, Hannah, you sound like you're about to start a military campaign," Scott said.

"That's no way to find love," Cassie said.

"She's right," Louise said. "I don't know about the universe knowing when the time is right, but guys can sense it when you're desperate, and they run. Right, Scott?"

"You might as well have a trio of redneck brothers standing behind you with shotguns."

"I'm not desperate," I said. "I'm organizing. The universe helps those who help themselves. I can't expect the guy to just turn up on my doorstep one day, can I? Don't you all want to find your soul mates?"

A silence descended around the table, a pocket of quiet amid the voices and dish-clattering of the restaurant.

"Well, yeah, I want to find him," Louise finally said. "But how?"

"That's what I'm going to figure out."

Three

Gypsy Scarf

"You keeping busy?" Robert asked, handing me the armload of pants and jackets that needed hemming. Robert was a salesclerk at Butler & Sons, an expensive sportswear shop where I got a lot of alterations work. He was six years older than me, tall and slightly overweight, with a fresh face that lit up whenever I came in. I suspected he had a crush on me, but I couldn't quite come to grips with the idea of dating a guy in his mid-thirties who still worked retail. Ambition and confidence were attractive, and Robert had neither.

Or maybe he didn't have a crush, and was just happy to see someone fairly near his own age. The clothes Butler & Sons sold looked as if they were meant for golfers and the country club set, or whatever passed for the country club set in Portland. The customers who came in for the taupe pants and boxy argyle sweaters were not likely to be young single women.

"Pretty busy," I said, taking the clothes. "I've got three appointments lined up for this afternoon."

"Have you had a chance to eat?" he asked.

I avoided his eyes. Any mention of food was a danger

sign. It seemed to go back to some primitive time when Man bring Woman meat, good, eat, eat. Which was fine, if Woman want Man, Man kill many mammoth, make good fire. Not fine, if Man kill one old pigeon and have wet wood. I wanted a good provider.

"Joanne usually feeds me," I said, which was pretty much the truth. She was my next appointment, and she usually did have muffins or coffee cake she encouraged me to eat. It wasn't a meal in the traditional sense, but I'd been counting on it as lunch.

"Oh." His face fell, and then he struggled to put the cheer back into his expression. "Maybe next week we can grab something to eat together. The food court has some pretty good stuff."

I smiled, rather painfully. "We'll see."

It was as good as I could do, for a response. It was neither dashing nor encouraging his hopes, although dashing was what I knew I should do. "You have to be cruel to be kind," and all that, which I think is almost harder on the dasher than on the dashee. But I got a lot of business at this store, and didn't want to create bad feelings with an employee.

Maybe he'd get the hint when I was too busy next week, and the week after, and then we could both pretend he had never expressed anything but friendly interest.

Butler & Sons was in the lower level of Pioneer Place Two, the new addition to the upscale shopping center in the heart of downtown Portland. Pioneer Place Two was connected to its older twin by a sky bridge and an underground tunnel, and it was along this tunnel that I walked with my armload of sportswear, following the streamlike undulations of decorative blue glass under my feet. The stores on either side were mostly the same chains found in every other city: the Body Shop, Victoria's Secret, the Gap, Banana Republic, Eddie Bauer. I much preferred to go to Saks to steal my ideas for clothes to make. Somehow everything looked just a little more beautiful there.

The tunnel came out in the lower level of the original Pioneer Place, in the atrium center where switchbacks of escalators rose up four floors to a skylight roof. Thirty-foot bamboo grew in enormous pots, and smooth oak benches curved around a fountain that bubbled from several spouts, the sound rebounding off the bare floors and the glass walls of the surrounding shops. For some inexplicable reason someone had thrown a bright red toothbrush into the fountain, to lie at the bottom amid the pennies and dimes.

I spotted a rack of *Willamette Week,* and lay the clothes over the back of a bench as I took a copy and sat to peruse the back pages. It's a weekly paper, the main alternative to the more run-of-the-mill *Oregonian.* No one I knew actually read the articles: all we wanted was the entertainment section and the personal ads. What I wanted today was found in the last few pages: ads for singles' activity clubs.

''Women Call Free! Meet Quality Singles Like Yourself!'' This, written above a heart with a photo of a blond woman seductively talking into a phone.

What women are willing to call those numbers? And what men do they find on the line? It was hard to not think of the ''slimers'' Louise talked about, who called the crisis line: men who would call up and pretend to need counseling, but there was always a telltale hitch in their voices that said they were jacking off. Apparently all they needed was a woman's voice to get them to blow weenie phlegm into their hankies.

"Summer Fun! Rafting! Hiking! All Singles!" another of the ads read, over a black-and-white photo of young, handsome people screaming in delight as they shot the rapids, water splashing up around their rubber raft, their paddles raised, their life jackets turning them into uniform human cubes of athletic enthusiasm.

This sounded much more like what I was looking for, but I had a feeling there was going to be a hefty membership fee. If I couldn't afford health insurance, I couldn't afford to fork over hundreds to go rafting with other desperate singles.

No, not "desperate," I reminded myself. Organized.

But still, there was something I didn't like about the idea of paying a membership fee. It seemed so...forced. I wanted to be organized, but I also wanted to preserve a bit of the illusion that I would meet Mr. One-in-a-Million by fortuitous chance.

I flipped back through the pages toward the Culture section, stopping briefly in the personals at Men Looking For Women, but then deciding to save that entertainment for later.

The Culture section had everything from music clubs to art gallery listings, and went on for pages and pages. I browsed through it and found a college production of Shakespeare's "Cymbeline", performed on the Reed College lawn; a jazz group scheduled for a night at Pioneer Courthouse Square; and myriad events that made me feel like I was getting old. They sounded so *loud.* And smoky. Ugh.

I bought an *Oregonian* for its Friday pull-out A&E section, and found a hike along a trail in the Columbia Gorge, organized by Portland Community College, to observe spring wildflowers and wildlife. Five dollars, bring your own lunch and water to the specified meeting point.

They all held possibilities for meeting a man, although you can't talk during a play. I might be able to drag Louise or Cassie along with me to the jazz night at Pioneer Courthouse Square, but I didn't really like jazz. But guys seemed to, so maybe. The hike—maybe, although my hunch was that guys would prefer to think of themselves as the type of outdoorsmen who didn't need a guide.

On the other hand, wouldn't it be nice to find someone who enjoyed nature for reasons other than shooting deer and drinking beer by the fire?

I'd always liked those naturalists on television, the men who talked with calm, knowledgeable assurance, and had the patience to wait for hours behind a bit of shrubbery for the chance of seeing an otter or black bear. Any guy who would go on a guided nature walk in the gorge had to be a nice guy.

Some instinct had me glance up from the paper, and there was Robert, not fifteen feet away, headed for the second tunnel that led to the food court. He turned his head and saw me, and I felt my cheeks heat. I smiled weakly at him, feeling like a dog caught eating the cat's food, and he gave me an uncertain little wave and then kept going.

Damn. He probably thought I'd been lying about the appointments, to avoid eating with him. I folded up the *Willamette Week* and the A&E section, and picked up the clothes, feeling like a clod. I shouldn't have dawdled here, when I knew there was the danger of his coming by and seeing me. Stupid, stupid.

Why did emotions have to create so many delicate webs of pain, so easy to blunder through? And how many would be destroyed, both my own and others, by the time I'd found my Mr. Right?

Maybe there was a reason love and war were so often mentioned together. In both cases, the casualties were legion.

"This is you, the Page of Wands," Cassie said, pointing to the tarot card in the center of the layout. We were sitting on the floor of Louise's eighth-floor apartment, later that same day. Louise had invited us over to dinner, and Scott would be coming by in time for dessert. The apartment was filled with the scent of baking lasagne, likely made with five or six exotic cheeses and half a dozen vegetables I'd never heard of. Louise liked to try recipes from trendy cookbooks.

Louise was already looking more healthy now that she was working days: the shadows were gone from beneath her eyes, and her skin had a touch of color beneath her darkening freckles.

Louise's apartment is in a new-ish building in the heart of downtown, the rent partially subsidized by her well-off parents, who slept better at night knowing that their daughter was in a safe place, with security cameras in the halls and a man at the desk in the lobby. Coun-

selors at crisis lines did not make much money, and
Louise would be living somewhere like I did if not for
her parents. I envied her modern bathroom and the bal-
cony with a view, but I liked where I lived with Cassie
and wasn't sure I'd trade.

"Why the Page of Wands?" I asked Cassie.

"Pages are for young women with lots of creative
energy. They tend to be action-oriented."

"Okay." I shuffled the deck, the oversize cards awkward in my hands, and then Cassie laid them out in what
she called the "gypsy spread." My question for the
cards was what my love life would be like in the next
four months.

"These cards on either side of you represent aspects
of yourself," she said. "Seven of Swords—you have
plans, but don't know how to put them into effect, or
whether they will succeed or fail. The Emperor—you
are taking action in the real world."

"That fits well enough."

Cassie looked up at me with a grin, henna-red hair
loose and slightly tangled, that and her elflike eyes making her look very much the part of the fortune-teller.
Louise sat to one side, arms crossed over her chest, ob-
serving with a half smile on her lips. She claimed to not
believe in spirits or supernatural forces, and said that the
only useful thing about tarot cards was that they served
as a good projective test for people's psyches. You saw
in the pictures what your personality allowed you to see,
and nothing more.

Me, I chose to believe the cards only when they told
me what I wanted to hear.

Cassie went through the aspects of the past that had

brought me to the present situation, and then the "forces beyond my control." Among them was a card with an angel standing with one foot on the ground, one in the water.

"Temperance," Cassie said. "Sometimes this means that your angel is near, helping to guide you."

"She is?"

Cassie shrugged. "You would know better than I. The interpretation of the cards is more for you to figure out than me."

"Do you believe in guardian angels?" I asked, curious. I didn't, but why then did I always get teary-eyed when I watched *Touched by an Angel* on Sunday nights? That I liked that show was one of my most closely guarded secrets.

"Sometimes I can feel my grandmother watching over me," Cassie said.

"Really?"

"Yes, really. She talks to me in my dreams, too."

"Huh." I didn't know quite what to say to that. I turned to the psychological expert. "What do you think, Louise?"

She shrugged. "If it is comforting and does no harm, there's no reason a person cannot believe what they wish."

"I thought counselors referred to that type of thinking as delusional," I said.

"In psychology, we say that no personality trait or behavior is a problem unless it causes problems for the client."

I chewed that over for a minute. "I guess that makes sense."

"Then again, some people are just plain nuts."

"That's very helpful, Ms. Counselor." I turned my attention back to the cards.

"These here represent the natural course of future events," Cassie said. "There is friendship and merriment, and learning to feel your emotions. Next are scattered energies, struggles. And here, the final card, the Ace of Swords. Change. Major change."

The Ace of Swords was a picture of a fist holding up a silvery-blue blade, with a crown and greenery circling the tip. "What type of change?"

"Could be good or bad. It's a card of new force, new energy, new direction. It's something dramatic, either positive or negative, and could be either love or hatred."

"But which is it?"

Cassie just looked at me, letting me flail about, looking for my own interpretation.

"Well, what are these other cards, then?" I asked impatiently, pointing to the three in the upper left-hand corner of the layout.

"Those represent other possible futures." She described the first two, then stopped at the third and gave me a meaningful look. "The Magician. He brings messages from the realms of the gods, often in the form of synchronicity. Watch for coincidences in your life, for there will be valuable information hidden therein."

"I don't know what any of that means," I said. "None of it sounds like a possible future." I was still feeling disgruntled about that Ace of Swords, and disinclined to give a generous interpretation to the cards. Hatred or love, change for the positive or change for the negative—huh! Very helpful, thanks so much!

"It is for you to decide what they mean," she said.

I continued to study the cards, unhappy that some of them seemed to fit my situation so well, while others did not. I wanted it all to be garbage, or all to be true. I don't enjoy ambiguity.

She let me stare at the cards a little longer, then scooped them up and put them back in the deck, wrapping the deck in a blue silk scarf. "You can make of it what you will," she said, "but at least look for synchronicities in your life. Whenever I get The Magician, strange things seem to happen, and I usually learn something from them."

"What types of strange things?"

"Oh, like maybe I've chosen five books at random from the fiction shelves at the library, and when I take them home and read them I discover that they all have a villain who looks and acts like Teddy Roosevelt."

"What on earth could you possibly learn from that?"

"It's like the cards. You can find the parallel in your own life, if you look for it. Maybe I'm dating a guy who reminds me of Teddy Roosevelt in some way, and the synchronicity is telling me that he is bad for me, that he's a villain. I don't know. It depends."

"Cassie, sometimes you're a very weird chick, you know that?"

"Am I?" she asked, sounding pleased.

"Definitely."

Louise got up and went to the refrigerator, returning with a two-liter bottle of Diet Pepsi. She refilled our glasses. "Have you outlined a plan of attack for finding Mr. One-in-a-Million?" she asked, capping the bottle and setting it on the coffee table, then sinking cross-legged onto the carpet.

"Somewhat." I told her about the events I'd found in the papers, and asked if she'd want to go to the free concert in Pioneer Courthouse Square.

"Jazz? I don't know," Louise said. "Maybe Cass will go with you."

"No way," Cassie said. "Guys who like jazz take themselves way too seriously."

"Or you might be able to get Scott to go," Louise said.

"What would be the point of going to a concert to meet guys, if I'm with a guy already? No one would approach me."

"Oh. That's right."

"Maybe I'll just do the gorge hike. Even if I did find a single guy at the jazz concert, he'd probably make me a tape of his favorite music, and then be all disappointed when I didn't like it."

"They're so cute when they try to share," Cassie said.

"I was also thinking of trying Internet dating. It seems like an efficient way to look for what you want. Sort of like shopping."

Louise made a face. "Are you sure about that? It's kind of dangerous, isn't it?"

"I shouldn't think it was any more so than meeting someone at a dance club."

"But people can lie when they're hidden behind their computers," Louise said.

"They can lie in real life, too. I've looked at a couple of the sites, and they seem pretty safe. You get a code name, and they give you a mailbox on the site, so no one has your real e-mail address.''

''I don't know, Hannah, you hear all sorts of stories...''

''You hear good stories, too.'' I lowered my voice to a confidential, persuasive level. ''Aren't you even a little bit curious about it? There might be a college professor or an artist on there right now, just the type you're looking for.''

''You don't want *me* to try it, do you?'' she asked.

''Why not? We all could, you, me, Cassie and Scott. You'd do it, wouldn't you, Cassie?''

''Yeah, sure, for a lark. Why not? I see plenty that goes on at the pub, and I wouldn't mind having a computer screen between me and some of the snakes out there while I'm looking for a date.''

''Some of the sites are free,'' I continued, ''and others give you a trial membership. Think of how many 'possibles' we could sort through, from the comfort of our own homes! And if they're all weirdos, we don't have to meet any of them in person.''

''I don't know...''

''Come on, it'll be fun.''

''If you can get Scott to do it, too, then maybe I will.'' She sounded far more reluctant than enthusiastic.

I grinned, victory within my grasp. ''This is going to be great.''

''Is it?'' Louise asked weakly, and reached for the bottle of Diet Pepsi.

''It'll be an adventure!''

''Wonderful.''

Four

Black Leather

"Hey, Hannah, you should have stopped by my office today," Scott said, closing our front door behind him. It was three days after our dinner at the restaurant. "This woman came in with an abscess under one of her molars. The infection went all the way down into the jaw, where it had eaten out a pocket of bone—"

"Oh, God, Scott, shut up!" I said, covering my ears and ducking my head toward my lap in an effort to shut out the image he was conjuring.

"I had to drill through her tooth, and when I did, this spurt of pus—"

"I'm going to throw up."

"And the smell—"

"Stop it!"

"I second that," Cassie said. "That is beyond gross. Jeez, Scott, you've been sucking ether too long if you think that makes interesting conversation."

"We don't use ether. That went out in the fifties."

"You get my point." She put her hand on my shoulder. "It's safe, Hannah. The beast has been silenced."

I glared at Scott, then spun ninety degrees in my desk

chair and stood, going to snatch the grocery bag out of Scott's hands. "What's in here?" I asked.

"Greedy thing, aren't you?"

"You went to Zupan's? We'll have to get out the linen tablecloth." Zupan's was the aesthetically pleasing grocery store a few blocks down from our house. Cassie and I usually shopped at Safeway, assuming that any supermarket as attractive as Zupan's must be beyond our means.

"That's me, Dr. Deep Pockets. I picked up some things to make this torture more endurable."

I dug through the bag. Purple grapes, store-made brownies, red wine and Tater Tots. I pulled out the bag of frozen potato product and held it up, making a questioning face.

"Don't you like Tater Tots?" Scott asked.

"Don't they remind you of school lunches from grade school?"

"If you don't want any, it's more for me."

Cassie took the bag from my hand and carried it into the kitchen. I heard banging as she dug out our one cookie sheet.

"Did you get the photos scanned?" I asked.

"I e-mailed them to you," he said, flopping down onto the lumpy futon with its stained blue-canvas cover. He looked perfectly at home. Our nasty beige shag carpeting never kept him from sitting on the floor, either, and it didn't seem to bother him that half our glasses were jelly jars.

I would say that was because he was a guy, but I'd seen his place, a condominium on a bluff overlooking NW Portland, and I knew better. His taste went toward black leather furniture and lots of stereo equipment, and he had recently purchased a mission-style cherrywood dining table.

Of course, all his furniture was buried under dirty clothes, magazines, dishes, and the unnamed effluvia of male existence, but the finer things were there, underneath. He'd once explained that he had to be so clean all day at work, he couldn't stand to extend the effort to his home.

That was dentists for you. Bunch of weird-os.

Louise showed up, her dark brown hair flying in wild curls around her head, tossed by the wind. The touch of pink in her cheeks made me realize anew how pretty she was, and my eyes went to Scott, wondering if he ever regretted that things had not worked out between them.

He seemed more interested in snooping through our bookshelf. I wondered whether he'd mention the guide to tantric sex that Cassie had recently added.

"Hannah, I think I got another client for you," Louise said.

"Oh?"

"Derek, at work. He's lost a bunch of weight and needs some suits altered. I gave him your card."

"Is he the one who just got divorced?"

"Uh-huh," she said, and the corner of her mouth crooked in a smile.

I raised my eyebrows. Scott stopped browsing the bookshelf, and Cassie appeared from the kitchen doorway, plate of Tater Tots in hand.

"What?" Louise asked.

"You tell me," I said.

"What? About Derek?"

"Don't say you're going for a guy who just got divorced," Scott said.

"I'm not! Who said I was? I'm not interested. He has two teenage kids, you know. He's too old for me." She smiled like a naughty child. "Looks pretty good since he lost that weight, though. Oh, I'm just kidding," she said before any of us could say anything. "You think I'm stupid? I have a degree in this crap, I know what not to do."

Cassie put the plate of Tater Tots down on the coffee table. "You're the one who told us that counselors were the most screwed up bunch of people on the face of the planet, and not worth dating."

"That's true enough."

I went over to the computer and woke it from sleep mode as Louise shed her coat and Cassie poured her a jelly jar of red wine. Scott went to work on the Tater Tots, squirting ketchup in a big puddle, and Cassie sat lotus-style and straight-backed on the floor and picked up a brownie. No one had touched the grapes, perhaps because they were fresh and unprocessed and therefore good for one. I tore off a small bunch and took them with me back to the computer desk, a few feet from the coffee table, just so they wouldn't look scorned.

"I don't have to write my own ad, do I?" Scott asked as I connected to the Internet. "You three should write it for me. You know what women want."

I peered at him over my shoulder. "The idea here is to find your one-in-a-million match, not to score as many babes as you can."

"That sucks. Maybe I'm not ready for my one-in-a-million."

"Yes you are," Louise said. "You've been messing around long enough."

"No I haven't. I just got the BMW six months ago. I need to cruise! I need to impress chicks with my wheels!"

"What are you, sixteen?" I asked.

"I need to put the top down and leer at women on the sidewalks. I need to have hot tub parties."

"You don't have a hot tub," I said.

"And your car is not a convertible," Louise said. "And this is Portland. Who has a convertible? It rains too much."

"Don't spoil my fun."

"Don't you ever wonder what germs might live in hot tub water?" I asked as I logged onto the personals site I had chosen for our group experiment. "You think of hot tubs at apartment complexes, and what scungy people might get in there nude, oozing fluids left and right. And then it just stays there, bubbling. Don't bacteria multiply in the heat?"

"Hannah, yuck," Cassie said. "I was going to go to Carson Hot Springs next weekend, too."

"Half a cup of Clorox might help," Scott said.

Cassie grimaced. "That's just what I want, to breathe in steaming bleach. That is not why one goes to natural springs."

"It's probably hot enough you don't really have to worry about anything," he said, and popped a Tot into his mouth.

"Okay, here we are," I said. "Who wants to go first?"

Louise came to stand behind me. "Let's look at some of the ads before we begin."

"Men or women?"

"Guys. I've got to see if there's anyone even worth bothering about."

I clicked my way to the search page, and filled out the obvious criteria of age range and marital status. "We can search by words in the ads, too."

"'Vegetarian,'" Cassie said.

"No!" Louise and I said in unison. "No vegetarians," I said.

"Why not?"

"They're high-maintenance eaters," I said.

"Thanks a lot."

"Oh, Cass, you're fine, you don't make a fuss. But for dating—I don't want some guy taking me to organic restaurants. And how could I bring a vegetarian home to Mom and Dad?"

Scott paused in his Tater consumption. "They'll only let you marry a carnivore?"

"Omnivore. It would just be too embarrassing. Can you see it? 'Sorry, Dad, Jeremy won't be eating any barbecued spare ribs. Could you grill this soy burger for him?' I'd never hear the end of it."

Cassie was still looking pouty. "I don't see why you should be embarrassed for someone else's eating habits. If he's fine with it, you should be, too."

"I'm too immature to separate my identity from my date's," I said.

"As if maturity had anything to do with it," Louise said. "None of us can do that. I certainly can't."

"That's a chick thing," Scott said. "Guys don't care what a girl eats, or what others might think of her taste in clothes, or anything like that."

"Bullshit," Louise said.

"Louise!" I said, rounding my lips in fake horror at her language.

"We don't!" Scott insisted.

"What a load of crap," Louise said. "You guys care, you just choose different criteria."

"We do not."

Louise nodded her head, bouncing it up and down like a street fighter getting ready to brawl, her jaw thrust forward. "You want your date to have big breasts and long hair. You want her to have a nice butt that other guys will stare at."

"Hey, that's got nothing to do with image."

"Sure it does," I said, catching Louise's thought. "The better-looking your girlfriend, the more of a 'man' you appear. You could look like a dead possum yourself, but if you had a beautiful woman on your arm other guys would assume you were something special. Even other women would assume it. They'd think you were rich. Either that, or..."

"Or what?"

"Never mind."

"Or *what*, Hannah?"

"You know." I cast a quick glance at his crotch.

Louise affected a Texas drawl. "They'd think that was a mighty fine cut of swinging sirloin you had between them thar legs."

"Of course, I wouldn't know anything about that type of thing," Cassie said, "being a vegetarian."

I spoke primly. "Some girls eat meat, some don't."

Scott gaped at us. "And they say guys are bad. You three are worse than any group of men."

"Oh, we are not," Louise said, swishing her hand dismissively.

"My privates are not up for discussion."

"You were the one who insisted," I said. "And why is it always referred to as a meat product? Sausage, salami, meat, sirloin, and having sex is 'porking.'"

"Because you women are the ones who spend all your time discussing it. In centuries past you were all in the kitchen. With the meat."

"Yep, that's where we were. Toiling with the meat," I said, and giggled, and saw Cassie and Louise bury their noses in their jelly jars. "But bread would have done as well. 'My man's got a fine loaf.' I could see that. 'I was up kneading it all night.'"

"It wouldn't rise," Louise said. "I put it in a warm place, but nothing happened."

"Maybe my yeast wasn't fresh," I said.

Cassie groaned. "Yeast. Oh, gross."

"I know, I'm terrible."

"You're as bad as Scott," Louise said.

He spoke around the last of the Tater Tots. "Hey, I contributed nothing to this line of discussion."

"You're guilty by association," Louise said. "You two should write a horror novel together. You could sit for hours thinking up revolting images."

"Only if the monster was a dentist," I said.

"He could never fit his hairy paws into his patients'

mouths," Scott said. "He could carry off an ornery seamstress, though."

"Yeah, right," I said, and turned back to the computer, suddenly feeling awkward and wanting to change the subject. "We're never going to get anything done at this rate."

Sometimes I got the littlest bit flustered around Scott. I knew he wasn't flirting with me, I knew that, yet when a cute guy makes a comment about carrying you off, you start wondering things you have no business wondering about your best friend's ex-boyfriend.

"Put in 'cooking,'" Louise said.

"Okay." I hit Search, and a few seconds later a list of names came up, some with a small camera beside them to denote a photo. "Here we go." I clicked on the first name with a picture as Scott and Cassie joined us at the computer.

A blank square came up, then the picture started to fill in, top to bottom.

"A tree, so far so good," Scott said.

The top of a head appeared, dark-haired, then a forehead. A face, long and narrow. Neck. Shoulders.

"Wait a minute," Scott said. "Is he *in* the tree?"

Louise put her hand over her mouth, laughing, as his lower body formed, and we could see his feet bracing him in position in the Y of tree branches. "What the hell kind of message is that supposed to send?" Louise asked. "'I am a squirrel'?"

"It's kind of cute," Cassie said. "Makes him seem boyish and playful."

"Thirty-four, software engineer—of course—never married, no kids, blah, blah, blah," I said, reading, then hitting the scroll bar to move past the bare stats to the paragraph Squirrel Boy had written about himself.

"'Handsome, fit, creative professional seeks an active, petite woman to share wild times and walks on the beach,'" I read, then groaned along with the rest. "Walks on the beach, why do they always talk about walks on the beach? Strolls in the moonlight, candlelit dinners, snuggling in front of the fire. Why can't they show some originality?"

"Don't forget 'rainy nights,'" Scott said.

"Those are a step above. It takes a slightly finer aesthetic sense to appreciate rain."

"What does he mean by 'petite'?" Louise asked. "Does he mean short, or skinny?"

I scrolled back up to the stats. Squirrel Boy was five-eight, one hundred and thirty-five pounds. "I'm guessing both. I don't know many guys who want their date to be bigger than they are."

"Skinny guys sometimes like plump women," Scott said. "It's no good having your bones rubbing against hers."

I frowned at him over my shoulder.

"Don't look at me like that. Most guys I know would rather have a girl with a little extra on her, than too little. You need something to hold on to."

Cassie nudged me from the other side. "I told you so. You can't be a good belly dancer without any belly. It looks wrong. Women are supposed to be soft."

"Mmm." I was not convinced. I wanted to be convinced, I would dearly love to believe those extra ten pounds were beautiful, but I would have to isolate myself from the rest of the U.S. to believe it.

I had a disturbing inkling that even if ten pounds were to fall off overnight, I would still think ten more needed to go. And then there were the two acne scars on my cheek I'd want lasered off, and the chin tuck, and the electrolysis for those nasty hairs around my navel and—horror upon horrors—my nipples. There was no end to the improvements to be made.

"This one's boring," Louise said. "Let's look at someone else."

The next photo was of a buff-looking guy leaning against a polished pickup, the sun glaring off the fenders and his sunglasses. His jeans were tight enough that the bulge of his penis was visible.

"Full of himself. Next," Louise said, not even giving me time to scroll down to read what the guy had to say.

A balding guy, going to fat, crouching down next to a Labrador. "Maybe," Louise said.

Scott made a noise of disbelief. "Him?"

"It's the dog," Louise explained. "Makes him look caring."

"Remind me to get a pet. A cat would be good. They're independent, not much trouble."

"Don't get a cat," I said.

"Why not?"

"Guys with cats are weird."

"Oh, for God's sake. Why?"

"They just are. They start talking about 'kitty did this' and 'kitty did that', and it's just wrong. Besides, your apartment will smell like dirty litter, and that's nothing to bring a girl home to."

"She's right, there," Louise agreed. "The way you

keep house, you're better off with... Huh, I can't think of anything that wouldn't eventually smell.''

''We're going to be here all day if you two keep looking through ads. Come on, let's get going.''

''Ooo, you're such a man,'' I said. ''So task-oriented.''

''That's me.''

Nevertheless, I could see his point, and over Cassie's and Louise's protests I clicked through to the ad-writing screen. ''Who first?''

''I'll go,'' Cassie said. ''I've got to get ready for work in a bit.''

I slid out of the desk chair and Cassie took my place. I went and sat at the other end of the futon from Scott, snatching another bunch of grapes on my way.

''There's a problem with your one-in-a-million mate theory, at least as it applies to Portland,'' Louise said, sitting in our battered old rocking recliner, rescued from a neighbor's yard sale.

''What's that?''

''Proximity. There may be two million people in the greater Portland area, but that covers a lot of space. Studies have shown that we tend to get involved with, and marry, those who live closest. Take two dating couples, one who lives twenty miles apart, and the other who lives five miles apart, and the five-milers are more likely to wed.''

''Where did you hear that?'' I asked.

''I've been reading up on it.''

''Makes sense,'' Scott said, working on the brownies now, one leg crossed over the other in that knees-wide position used only by men. "It's a lot less bother to pick a girl up five minutes away, than half an hour."

"You're so romantic," I said. "Sounds like you'd walk through fire for your true love."

He shrugged, brownie in hand. "It's the truth. Men are lazy slobs. You should know that by now."

"So the point is," Louise said, "if it's only the closest people we can fall for, then we aren't really searching all of the greater Portland area, which means less of a pool."

I chewed my lip, considering. "No, I don't think that's a problem. The idea was not that there would be one million single guys our age who wanted to get married: it was that there were one million males. We're already draining away most of the pool just by selecting for age and marital status. So we drain out a few more by location. No problem. Although I admit, it sounds like the pool is turning into one of those shallow mud baths the zebras wallow in during the dry season."

Cassie looked over her shoulder. "Welcome to the dating world."

The Serengeti image was strangely appropriate, and put a bit of a damper on my enthusiasm for the project. I'd briefly managed to see Portland as a vast uncharted sea of men, but now I was back to the mud wallow.

"What else have you been discovering?" I asked Louise, in hopes of something cheering. She had a mini psychology library in her apartment, and between that and working with fifty-odd counselors and social workers, she usually had good access to interesting information. She was enough of a cynic about life and love that she was constantly looking for a scientific explanation for personal things that the rest of us took for granted.

"Along with the proximity, is familiarity. It's not that we know what we like—we like what we know. So the more time you spend with someone, the better you like them."

"Doesn't that work the opposite way?" Scott asked.

I made a face at him. He grinned.

"Same thing happens with music, or a piece of art," Louise explained. "Or fashion. You ever notice how when something new comes out, you swear you will never wear it, and then six months later it's in your closet."

"Unfortunately," I agreed.

"Then there's similarity," Louise went on. "Age, race, ethnic background, educational level, social status, family background, religion."

"I can see that. Less to argue about," I said. "Less to get adjusted to. And if you got involved with the person because they lived close by, you probably have a lot in common already."

"Social status?" Cassie asked, turning away from the monitor. "You mean, like class differences? Where are we, India?"

Cassie was maybe the one person I knew who I could imagine being equally comfortable in the company of a drug addict who had dropped out of middle school or a middle-aged society matron from the West Hills. She was so firmly in her own world, the relative positions of others could not shake her.

There were times I hoped I would grow up to be like Cassie.

"And last but not least," Louise went on, "physical attractiveness."

"Hoo-rah!" Scott said.

"Oh, stop it," Louise scolded. "You're not nearly the animal you think."

"Ha. What do you know?"

"You're a 'nice guy,'" I said, feeling wicked. "You're the type that women like to have as a friend."

"Kee-rist! Thanks a lot! Could you be a little more insulting?"

I gave a toothy grin.

"When's the last time you had a checkup? Maybe it's time for some dental X rays."

"Don't be mean." Memories of hard cardboard edges poking my gums filled my mind, and the heavy weight of the lead apron on my chest. The smell of alcohol, the taste of the latex-gloved fingers against the edge of my tongue...

"The thing about the physical attractiveness," Louise said, "is that we go for someone as attractive as we think we can get without risking rejection."

"That must be why handsome men are so terrifying," I said.

"I scare you that much?" Scott asked.

I snorted.

"Come on, Scott, you're the same way," Louise said. "I've been with you when you've refused to approach a woman because you thought she was too beautiful for you."

That was interesting. I never thought of Scott thinking himself not good enough for anyone. Who wouldn't want a good-looking guy who was a reliable provider? What did he have to be uncertain about?

"You know," I said, "you see rich, ugly men with beautiful women, but you never see a rich, ugly woman with a handsome man. Never. The closest you get is a famous, rich older woman with a young guy, but even then she's got to still be looking pretty good."

We looked at Scott.

"What? I didn't do anything."

"Guilt by association," I said.

"I thought I was a 'nice guy.'"

"So you'd date a woman less attractive than yourself?"

"That's not a fair question."

"Why not?"

"Because if I answer honestly, I'll sound like a pig."

"What's unfair about that?"

"You already know the answer. Everyone knows, you don't need a scientific study to prove it. Guys are visual. We want someone good-looking, if we can get her."

"And even if you can't," I said, beginning to get steamed by the injustice of it. I hated caring about my appearance as much as I did, I wanted to believe it didn't matter, that it was inner beauty that counted, but every time I almost started to convince myself of that, something came along to say I was wrong.

"I saw an interview on TV," I said, "with some guy who said his only intimate relationships were with prostitutes, because the women that he found attractive in daily life did not find him attractive in return. So he'd rather pay for it, and have it fake, than get to know a real woman he could maybe build a life with."

"For God's sake, Hannah. Now you're comparing me to a guy who sleeps with hookers? All I said was that I'd prefer someone attractive. So would you. So would anyone. Listen to Louise, she's the one who read the study!"

"I'm putting that in my profile," Cassie said. "'Must have no history of dating prostitutes.' Do you think that will put anyone off?"

The tension broke, and I relaxed back against the futon. Scott nudged my knee with his foot, and I slapped it lightly away, looking at him from the corner of my eye and not quite able to keep from smiling.

"If it does," Louise said, "it's just as well. Think of the diseases! Bleh!"

Five

Mourning Clothes

My mobile phone rang as I slowly cruised the residential street of tract mansions looking for Kristina De-Frang's house. She was a new client, referred by Joanne of the muffins and too much clothing.

I pulled to the curb and stopped before answering, having promised myself when purchasing the thing that I would not annoy the rest of humanity by driving and talking at the same time. I'd come near to breaking the promise a hundred times, and who would know? But I didn't want to be one of *those* cell phone users. I wanted to be one of the good ones, who when in public huddled in a corner and whispered a brief conversation, then hung up quickly.

Perhaps that was another criteria to put in the personal ad, besides no history of dating prostitutes: does not use mobile phone while browsing at Barnes & Noble or standing in line at Starbucks. Cassie would qualify that with: prefers independent businesses to chains, and does not know the difference between a Grande and a Tall.

I, on the other hand, thought Starbucks and Barnes & Noble were both good places to look for guys. Some

guys apparently thought the same thing about book-
stores: I'd once been followed aisle to aisle by a lum-
mox carrying a copy of *Chicken Soup for the Single's
Soul.*

"Hello, this is Hannah."

"Hannah! Are you on the phone?"

It took a daughter to translate Mother-speak correctly.
"Hi, Mom. I'm on the cell phone, in my car."

"You aren't driving, are you? Should I call back?"

"It's okay, I'm parked. What's up?"

"Where are you?"

"Nearly to Camas, looking for a client's house."
Camas was across the river, in Washington state, about
half an hour from Portland. "She's supposed to have a
big job for me, something about redecorating her second
house."

"Dad can't get the VCR to work."

The abrupt change of topic was nothing new, and I
tried to not take offense at her apparent lack of interest
in my work. And it *was* only an apparent lack: I knew
that she cared how I was and that I was able to make
ends meet, but the specifics of that struggle and of my
work were beyond her present life.

Mom and Dad were nearly seventy, having had me
late and as a bit of a surprise. Mom was a retired grade
school teacher, and Dad had been a carpenter and was
now a housing inspector. He talked about retiring, but I
doubted he would unless forced to. They lived in the
house I had grown up in, in Roseburg, three hours south
of Portland. It wasn't the boonies, but it was pretty
close.

"Put him on," I said.

There were scuffling sounds, muted voices, then Dad. "I followed your instruction sheet, but it didn't work, and now I can't get the regular TV stations, either. I think the remote's batteries need to be changed."

I stifled a sigh. How could a man who could spot the first faint signs of dry rot and tell the exact remaining life span of a roof be stymied by a couple of black buttons?

"Get the biggest remote..." I said, and within half a minute I heard the static disappear from the background, and the voice of a newscaster caught mid-drone.

"Thanks! I think I can remember how to do that," Dad said, and then Mom was on the phone again.

"He's rented some awful gangster movie. He knows I don't like those."

"What is it?"

"Analyze This."

"You might like it. It's a comedy."

"I don't know how gangsters can be funny."

"I gotta go, Mom, or I'll be late."

"Okay. When are you coming down for dinner?"

"I'll call from home. I really have to go."

"They've seen bears in the park, coming out to go through the garbage. The salmon berries are late in coming out this year."

"I gotta go, Mom!"

"Love you."

"Love you, too."

I hung up, feeling the mix of guilt and love and worry that I usually did after talking to my parents. In the back of my mind sat the realization that death or accident or illness was not just a possibility, but an inevitability. What would happen to one, when the other died?

What would happen to me?

I picked up the instructions to Ms. DeFrang's house, looked again at the address, and coasted down the street, trying not to think of the future.

Six

Silk vs. Spandex

"How much are you going to get for doing that job?" Louise asked, raising her voice to be heard over the shouts of juvenile delinquents. We were in the lobby of the Garland Theater, a one-time movie house that had decomposed into a venue for local bands and, twice a month, professional wrestling.

If you wanted to call it professional.

"I'll have to figure it out, but I'm guessing about fifteen hundred. You should have seen her place: it was in one of those big new housing developments where every house has something like four thousand square feet, yet they all have these dinky little bits of yard. You could reach out a window and shake hands with your neighbor."

"Who'd want to live in one of those? They all look alike."

"Yeah, I know, but this Kristina DeFrang's house, it was different. You went inside, and you wouldn't have known the house was brand new. You'd have thought Thomas Jefferson lived there, or King Louis the Something."

"Lots of antiques?"

"Yeah, but not like some people do, where there's Victorian junk clogging up all the space. This was...different. And it didn't look like any one particular style. Everything blended."

"Could have been in *House Beautiful?*" Louise asked.

"I wish I knew how to put together a room like that."

And I wouldn't mind someday being Ms. DeFrang. She was in her late forties, fit in that spalike way wealthy women look fit, but without the usual accompanying manacles of gold and diamonds on wrists and fingers. Her hair was cut in a bob similar to mine, and she wore minimal makeup. Her clothes were simple and obviously expensive, and I knew it would be beneath her dignity to show the name of a designer, or to sport a style that showed a hint of trendiness.

How she'd ended up in that nouveau neighborhood, I don't know. She seemed too good for it.

She was too good for me, too, but she was the type who would consider it a mark of bad breeding if she ever let her awareness of that show.

I'd felt like a tacky frump following her around her house, my shoes looking like the discount store copies they were, my pantyhose showing the coarseness of knit available only at the grocery store. My blouse I'd made myself, copying one I'd seen at Saks, but with its sleeves that belled at the wrist and the ruffle at the surplice neckline, it felt gauche when confronted with Ms. DeFrang's timelessness.

"She wouldn't be caught dead here," I said.

"Huh?"

"Ms. DeFrang. But if she had to come here, she'd make it look like she was pleased to be invited."

"Then she has more grace than I do. Why did I let you talk me into this? Remind me?"

"Ah, come on. You need new experiences," I said as we shoved our way into the theater and fought our way to our seats.

"No, I don't."

"You'll have a great story to tell," I said.

"If I survive."

"There are dads with their kids here. It's family fun!"

"They'll all grow up to be murderers."

We sat down, and I tucked between my feet the paper bag with the costume I was going to deliver.

"So she wants you to copy the entire master suite?" Louise asked, going back to Ms. DeFrang.

"The entire thing, only in different fabrics that she's ordering from her decorator. She and her husband have a house on Orcas Island, up in Puget Sound, with the same basic layout as the one in Camas. And she wants me to do the guest bedroom up there, too, that her mother-in-law uses."

"So, what is it, dust ruffles and duvets?"

"And about a dozen decorative pillows, and hangings for the beds. A lot of it is simple stuff, but the pillows are going to be a little tricky. They've got contrasting striped borders, piping that I have to make myself, mitred corners. They're going to be a pain. And I have to order the pillow forms myself, from a wholesaler."

"But that's why you get the big bucks."

"Oh, yeah, I'm rolling in it."

The announcer came out, a late middle-aged man with

a belly and light brown hair in a pompadour, his skin craggy and mottled. He started his spiel, trying—vainly, I thought—to add drama to the lineup of local wrestlers.

"The Logger, straight from the backwoods where they eat owls for dinner," he said, to a mix of cheers and boos from the crowd. "The Body Bag, and you know why he's called that—"

"He sends them home in a bag!" a kid to our right yelled.

"I can't believe you talked me into this," Louise said.

"We'll just wait until Elroy has his match, then go down to the dressing room." Elroy was my client, whose new spandex pants I had in the bag between my feet. I'd done costumes for a couple wrestlers down in Eugene when I'd worked at the alterations shop, and they'd passed my name along.

There was something perverse about it, but I had a bit of a thing for wrestlers. Not these locals sorts so much, but the ones on the WWF had a way of catching my eye. Those greased-up, muscled bodies throwing each other around called to something primal within me.

Not that I could see myself married to one of them. They were the toys of my imagination, and I was happy to keep them there, where their oiled locks wouldn't stain my pillows. Although maybe just once...

A round of cheers went up as the first wrestlers came out, one of them flanked by two women who looked as though they lived under a bar. The wrestlers were no more appealing, their bulk in their barrel chests coated with a layer of fat.

"My butt has better muscle tone than either of theirs," Louise said. "Don't these guys work out?"

"They always start the evening with the unknowns. The later guys will be a little more interesting."

"I can hardly wait."

Some of the young boys in the audience were getting excited by the match, shouting and booing, and there were some drunk college-age guys being obnoxious a few rows down. The rest of the house had a tired feel to it, as if seeing a porky guy in lace-up red boots being thrown onto a wrestling mat wasn't fine entertainment.

"I want to see some blood," Louise said. "Blood!" she said in a half shout.

The kid next to us heard her, and took up the cry. "Blood! Blood! Bust him open!"

The boy's father leaned around his son and gave us a dirty look. I shrugged helplessly, trying to look innocent. He shook his head and leaned back.

"He's not so bad," Louise said, nodding her head toward the father. "Is he wearing a wedding ring?"

"You're beginning to scare me."

"I kind of like this. Who here is going to care what I do?" She stood and started shouting toward the ring. "Headlock, baby! Jackhammer! Body slam!"

"What are you doing?" I hissed, yanking at the hem of her blouse. "Sit down! Louise!"

"Pile driver! Sit on him! Wooooo-hoo!"

"Louise! You're embarrassing me." I could feel my face going red as people turned to look.

"Put him in a granny hold!"

"Louise!"

"Wooooo-hoo!" she cheered, punching her fist into the air, then finally submitted to my tugging and sat as the match ended and new wrestlers came out. "That was fun."

"You were screaming nonsense."

"Yeah, so what? No one cares. Maybe they'll think I'm some kind of expert."

"I doubt it."

"Oh, lighten up."

"This isn't like you."

"What can I say? It's the testosterone in the air. I should get some of my co-workers to come here, for stress relief. God, I get so sick of having to watch every word I say."

"You mean on the phones?"

"You can't be flippant with suicidal callers or some guy whose wife just left him."

"I wouldn't think so," I said.

"But you know," she said, sounding thoughtful, "it's never the mentally ill I mind talking to. It's the walking wounded, the so-called normal people who drive me up a wall—especially family members of someone with a mental illness. God, they're annoying. And even off the phones—lately it seems like everyone who works at the crisis line is involved in their own petty political battles."

"Like what?"

She waved her hand dismissively. "Oh, I don't even know. Who gets to be a supervisor. How time off will be decided. Who gets to change their schedule. Whether someone screwed up on a call, and what should be done if they did. I feel like the only thing to do is to lie low and keep my mouth shut, and hope no one notices me."

"Is this all recent?"

"It's probably always been like this, I just didn't have to see it because I worked nights."

"You're not going to go back to that schedule, are you?"

She hesitated. "No. I like having a life."

"But?"

"But it was a lot more peaceful. I don't know. Maybe I'll start looking for another job. Derek is thinking of doing that, too."

"The divorced guy who needs his pants taken in? Just how much talking are you and Derek doing?"

"We had dinner last night."

"Louise!"

"Just dinner! It was just friendly, and we talked about work. I told him about the Internet thing, too."

"'Just dinner,' my ass. What'd he say about the personal ads?"

"Told me to be careful, of course."

"I don't think you need to worry. With that ad you put on, no one's going to answer," I said.

"I saw no reason not to ask for exactly what I wanted, if I was going to do this."

"Who's going to fit all those criteria?" Louise's ad had been two long lists of wants and don't-wants. "Wanted: over 5'10; master's degree or higher; aged 28-34; fit; omnivorous; reads fiction; can ballroom dance; knows how to cook at least three dishes worthy of being served to company; owns a car less than five years old; has traveled outside the country. Not wanted: smoking; drugs; excessive alcohol; divorcés; sexually transmitted diseases; either children or the desire to have children; snowboards; hunting; video games; trips to Las Vegas.''

"You said there's one in a million,'' Louise said.

"I think you don't want anyone to answer. Then you won't have to deal with dating.''

"I'm not against dating. I just don't feel the pressure you do.''

"Because you don't want to have children,'' I said. Louise had never been interested in having them, and for all any of us could tell, never would be.

"Probably.''

"Sometimes I think you don't want to get involved with anyone, period.''

She shrugged. "Maybe I don't. I miss the physical contact, but then I think about all the work that it takes to find someone you're willing to get to know, all the cruddy dates you have to go through, and then how long it takes to be sure enough of the person to be willing to open yourself to them, and... And suddenly a plate of lasagne and the TV start looking like a pretty good substitute.''

"I feel tired just listening to you.''

"There's more to life than sex and relationships.''

"Is there?'' I asked, smiling to show I was joking. Kind of.

"Work and love, that was what Freud said was important in life.''

"Then we still only have half.''

"But we can love our family, and our friends,'' she said, and blinked her eyes at me like a lovesick fool, and made kissing sounds.

"Great.''

I looked back at the ring just in time to see Vinnie the Hit Man's elbow accidentally go into The Snow Man's mouth. Blood spattered, and the Snow Man spit a glob of red mucous into his hand, and even from back where we sat I could tell that he'd found one of his teeth in that glob.

"Oh, God," I said, slapping my hands over my eyes.

"Hey, that doesn't look fake."

"It's not."

"Vinnie looks pretty embarrassed. Huh. Too bad Scott's not here. What are you supposed to do with a tooth that's been knocked out like that? Put it in a glass of milk?"

"I don't know," I said from beneath my hands. "I don't want to know."

"Wow. This is more exciting than I'd expected. Thanks for taking me!"

I groaned, and tried not to think of teeth.

Seven

Green Plaid

Dear Hannah,
It sounds like we have a lot in common. Would you be interested in meeting? Give me a call. My number is (503)555-8380.

Wade

"Cass, I've caught one!"

"Caught one what?" she called back from the kitchen, sounding worried. "Please don't say a cockroach."

"No, a man! Maybe a cockroach disguised as a man, but I'm hoping not."

That drew her out, a veggie burrito in her hand. She had on a black sports bra and a low-riding brown batik skirt, with a belt made of old coins ka-chinging around her hips. She'd been practicing dancing in our living room before hunger had struck.

"Which one is it?" she asked, coming to stand beside me at the computer.

"The wildlife biologist."

"Which one was he again?"

I reached for my binder and flipped pages. I'd gotten so many responses to my ad, the specifics of who was who had started to blend and I'd resorted to charting out the prospects.

"Thirty-six, brown hair, blue eyes, never married, moved here from Utah three months ago to work for the Audubon Society. He likes collecting old records, hiking, camping, the Discovery Channel, favorite movie is *The Hunt for Red October*—like me!—and favorite book is *Lord of the Flies*."

"That doesn't sound promising, *Lord of the Flies*."

"Why not? I love that book," I said.

"And you are a disturbed individual. Look at you and that binder."

"Hey, I'm on a mission."

"Love is not a mission," Cassie said.

"For me it is. Or maybe I should say 'business.'" I paused and considered. "Or maybe not. That doesn't sound quite like what I mean."

"Whatever."

"And there *is* a certain element of synchronicity to it: remember me talking about going on a nature hike with a guide? Look, I could have my own personal expert on hand!"

"Mmm," she said, not half as convinced as I thought she should be, considering that she was the one who said I should look for coincidences.

"Have you written back to anyone yet?" I asked.

She took another bite of burrito. "No."

"Cass!" I said, exasperated. "Why not?"

She shrugged. "None of them felt right."

"'Felt right'? It just feels unfamiliar, is all. I thought there were a few who had a lot in common with you."

"The energy was wrong."

I pursed my lips. I never did well with discussions of 'energy.' "Do you mean there was something suspicious about their profiles, or their letters? Or annoying, like those guys who claim to want a smart woman but misspell 'intelligent'?"

She shrugged one shoulder. "Maybe. I just don't feel that I'm going to find the right person on the Internet."

"And you won't, if you go at it that way."

"You never know. Love comes when you're not looking for it. You have to release your desires before you can achieve them."

I frowned at her, then turned back to the monitor. How could you not be looking for love, if you'd put an ad up? And how would you ever get what you wanted, if you gave up striving for it?

"Where are you going to meet him?" she asked.

"Someplace public. Maybe the Starbucks at Pioneer Courthouse Square. That should be safe, don't you think?"

"Should be. Just be careful."

"I'm not stupid. I won't get in his car or anything."

"Hannah, doesn't it seem a little wrong to you that we should even be having a discussion like this?"

"You mean, assuming that anyone we meet might be a psychopath?" I asked.

"Dating shouldn't be like this."

I chewed my bottom lip. My parents had met at a town picnic. How much more quaint could you get? There had been enough mutual acquaintances that they could each reassure themselves of the other's reputation. As far as I knew, Mom had never had to worry that Dad might haul her off into the woods, rape her, then leave her murdered body buried under a pile of leaves.

"I know it shouldn't," I said. "But what choice do we have?"

"There's always choice."

"Yes, well, I'm going to explore all the choices I've got. This is only one prong of my multipronged dating attack plan, you know."

"Do I." She started heading back to the kitchen. "Let me know where and when you decide to meet him. And leave me his name and number, just in case."

"Yes, Mother," I said, but was glad she'd asked. It felt a little better to know that someone would be keeping track of how long I was gone and where I was. It might be important when the police tried to track down my killer.

Cassie was right. There really was something wrong with dating like this.

Four days later I sat on a stool at the counter that lined the plate-glass windows, sipping chai. Starbucks was crowded with noon-time business people and semi-eclectic twenty-somethings. The coffee shop was perched above the northwest corner of Pioneer Courthouse Square, a red brick plaza often called "Portland's living room."

I had my back to the windows, and to the group of street kids who hung out there. White guys with dread-locks, wearing pullovers woven in Third World countries; girls with hair dyed bubblegum blue or ketchup red, with silver studs dotting their faces; wanna-be Maoris, their cheeks and noses swirled with green tattoos. I didn't know how any of them could hope to get a job, except maybe at faux-hip vintage clothing stores where funny-smelling garments were passed off as stylish and daring. Then again, jobs probably weren't their main concern just now.

The problem was, they reminded me too much of the college kids in Eugene. I'd finally reached the age where instead of such personal expression in dress seeming liberating, and possessed of some magic symbolism, it just seemed silly. And limiting. No one takes seriously a woman with a stud sticking out of her lower lip like a big steel pimple.

I took another sip of chai, watching the customers arrive and leave. I was ten minutes early for my meeting with Wade the wildlife biologist, and so had plenty of time to fret over which unsuitable guy might or might not be him.

He'd said he'd be wearing a tan coat, which I assumed was the basic color of a biologist trying to blend in with the background. He hadn't posted a photo with his ad, and hadn't had access to a scanner to e-mail one, so the only picture I had of him was in my head. I was imagining a broad jaw, broad shoulders, and creases at the corner of the eyes from squinting against the sun out in the wilds. And of course, a deep, slow voice like a narrator on a nature program.

I crossed my fingers for a quick second. Please let him have the voice. I'd heard it said that while a woman's most sexual feature was her hair, a man's was his voice. I loved it when you could feel the vibrations of a man's voice rumbling in your own chest: it was like he was becoming intimately acquainted just by speaking.

A man in khakis and a blue oxford shirt came in, brown hair, beige windbreaker over his arm. He got in line to place his order, eyes casually scanning the room, skimming over me, then his phone rang and he pulled it out of his pocket.

I watched him a few moments longer, but he showed no sign of looking for me, and a cell phone definitely did not fit my picture of Mr. Wildlife.

I wondered if, when Mr. Wildlife did show up, I would fit his expectations, in turn.

My own ad had run thus:

One in a million

I'm a confident, self-employed mistress of the seam who is looking for that one-in-a-million match. 29 yrs old, HWP, blond, blue-gray, and pretty without pretension. I love creating with my hands, spending time with friends, and exploring odd corners of the city and the countryside. My match would be 29-39 years old, no children (yet), happy in his chosen profession, with a spirit of adventure and yet preferring to walk on the tamer side of life—no drugs, heavy drinking, etc. etc., you know what I mean.

Originally I'd put "spirit of adventure" without any qualifiers, but Louise had warned that such a phrase might invite men with an interest in S&M.

I'd done a little playing with bondage in the past—

and had considered making my own Velcro wrist straps—but I certainly wouldn't want to date someone who was so into it that they searched for a woman based on such criteria. I tended to view with suspicion ads that asked for feminine women. What did a guy mean by "feminine"? Submissive? Eager to be told what to do? Weak?

I was getting paranoid. Most of them probably just meant she kept herself groomed and didn't engage in belching contests.

"Hannah?"

I turned, and felt my face flush, my heart suddenly thudding in my chest. "Wade?"

"I was hoping it might be you," he said, and held out his hand.

I slid down from my stool, switched my chai to my other hand, and shook, nerves overwhelming me and making my muscles quiver.

He wasn't what I had expected. He was just under six feet, his posture stooped, his frame narrow and with no hint of brawn. There was a faint resemblance to Anthony Hopkins in his face, if Anthony Hopkins had been in his thirties, still had his hair, and looked more frightened than frightening.

And the voice was average.

Still, he was not displeasing. He looked friendly.

"Did you have any trouble finding the place?" I asked, somewhat stupidly. This Starbucks was one of the easiest places in the city to find.

"Not much, although I got turned around trying to figure out all the one-way streets. I've only been downtown twice before," he said. "Last time I ended up going over three different bridges by accident."

"Three?" I asked, beginning to feel hopeful about this. Here was a guy who admitted getting lost, and was willing to laugh about it.

"I'd be on a street, driving along, then suddenly there was a railing and the river far below, and I'd be on the east side."

"It takes a while to get it all straight. Did you want something here?" I asked, gesturing to Starbucks at large.

"I was thinking, maybe, we could walk around a bit?"

"Okay."

I was too nervous to finish my chai, so I dropped it in the trash on the way out. He opened the door for me, then held it for another woman to go by, as well.

"Which way?" I asked.

"I don't know. I was hoping to wander and see some of the city."

"I could give you a mini walking tour," I said. "If you want."

"That'd be great."

We headed up Broadway to the Performing Arts Center, then cut between two of the buildings to the Park Blocks, which stretched south to the P.S.U. campus, the art museum and the Oregon Historical Society.

I snuck glances at him as I pointed out landmarks, taking in his T-shirt and old green plaid shirt, worn khakis and stained sneakers. It didn't look as though he'd taken much effort with his appearance.

Perhaps that was a good thing. He seemed easygoing,

and while he might not be exactly spiffy, at least he was clean and had short hair. He wasn't a slob. He was just used to the company of ducks and raccoons, that was all.

Unless it was all a disguise, and he really was a psychopathic serial killer. They were supposed to look innocuous, after all. Or like Anthony Hopkins.

Was this the type of synchronicity that Cassie had been talking about in my tarot card reading? God, I hoped not.

"How many dates have you had, off the Internet?" I asked as we headed toward the river, and Waterfront Park, which ran along its west bank. It was wide open and in the heart of downtown, so I needn't fear being dragged into any bushes.

"This is my first. And you?"

"Mine, too."

Nice guy, but I was beginning to feel as if I was doing all the conversational work. Maybe if I was quiet for a while he would start talking.

We walked in silence for several minutes, and then there was a faint stirring of sound from him. I waited, and then waited a little longer.

"Are you hungry?" he asked.

At last! He speaks! "A little. Are you?"

"A little. Do you know somewhere to eat?"

My spurt of excitement died. I didn't want to choose a restaurant—it was his turn to make a decision. But I also knew he'd only been in downtown Portland twice. I felt weary suddenly, and was tempted to say I had to go home, but then he looked at me, a shy smile on his lips, and I didn't have the heart.

"Do you like Thai?" I asked instead.

"Is it like Chinese?"

"Kind of."

"Okay."

Okay, then. Lunch.

"I got Mooch when I was collecting data for my thesis, in Colorado," Wade was saying.

Two minutes earlier, the check had arrived, and was now sitting inside its black folder at the edge of the table. Wade had made no move toward it.

"He was no bigger than the palm of my hand."

My glance slid to the folder. Should I reach for it? Pull it toward me and open the cover?

"His mother was a Burnese mountain dog, his father a German shepherd."

Wade had finally found a topic upon which to converse, and although he had glanced at the waiter when he brought the check, I wasn't certain that the significance of that event had imprinted itself upon his consciousness. I nodded and smiled and pretended to listen. Should I just say, "Dutch treat" and see how he reacted?

Should I just wait?

I had chosen the restaurant: did that mean I was expected to pay for both of us?

"He chewed the upholstery off the headrests in my car, so they're covered in duct tape now."

In a perfect world, he'd sweep the check into his hand and say, "Let me get it." Or better yet, say nothing at all, and without breaking the conversation slip his

MasterCard inside, as if money were too low a topic to let intrude.

I was fantasizing. I was a modern woman, I was supposed to want to pay my own way. It's not as though I was looking for free food.

Was I?

No, what I wanted was clear rules on what I was supposed to do. I didn't know what he expected, I didn't know what I expected, I didn't know what it would mean if he paid, if I paid, if we both paid. And he wasn't showing any signs of helping me out.

I couldn't stand it any longer. I reached for the folder.

His eyes blinked in surprise. "Oh, don't worry about that," he said, laying his hand on it and pulling it toward him. "I'll take care of it."

I smiled. The boy had potential.

Eight

Rubber Boots

"I don't get it. We've had three dates, and he hasn't so much as held my hand."

"Hey, this would be good for terrorizing hikers," Scott said, holding up a hunting knife.

We were in GI Joe's, an automotive and outdoors store. Scott was looking for a new bicycle pump, and I was looking for a pair of black rubber boots like I used to wear when I was in grade school.

"What do you think's going on with him? Is he not interested?"

"He asked you out again, didn't he?"

"Not yet, but he e-mailed."

"What exactly does a wildlife biologist do?"

"Rehabilitates wounded animals at the Wildlife Care Center. Leads birding field trips. And goes 'pish.'"

"'Pish'?"

I made the "pish" sound repeatedly, in demonstration. "Birds are supposed to like it."

"Do they come when you do it?"

"Not that I could tell. Wade looks kind of cute while he does it, though."

Scott led the way to the tent display, with its smell of synthetic fibers, sleeping bags spread out inside one of them. "Want to take a nap?" he asked.

"Tempting, isn't it? Louise always gets embarrassed when I try out the chairs and couches in furniture stores."

"I love her dearly, but sometimes she needs to loosen up," Scott said.

"You should have seen her at the wrestling match. I wouldn't be surprised to see her in the ring someday, taking out her built-up frustrations against annoying callers.

"Hey, check these out," I said, picking up a pair of binoculars and scoping out the store. I turned to look at him through them, a big blurry blob, then flipped the binoculars around and peered through the wrong end. "Dentist on the horizon! Man the cannon!"

"I like shopping with you," Scott said.

I lowered the binoculars. He was looking more serious than required for the tent department. "Do you?"

"Yes."

"Just because I'm willing to test the products for you, saving you valuable time and money," I said.

"Of course."

We wandered out of the tent display and found the rubber boots. Wade had invited me for a slog through one of his favorite wetlands, and I needed the appropriate footwear for the outing.

"Fourteen bucks," I said, picking out a pair of boots in my size. "Do you think Wade is worth it?"

Scott shrugged, picking up a pair of boots and sniffing

them, then putting them back on the metal shelf. "He sounds nice enough. But maybe he's…"

"Maybe he's what?" I asked, wondering why he'd sniffed the boot.

"A little too passive for you. Maybe you need someone more aggressive."

"I don't like macho guys."

"I don't mean macho. I just mean…someone who will make a move. Someone who won't let you push him around."

"I don't try to push people around. What, do you mean I'm bossy?" I asked.

"Didn't your last boyfriend accuse you of that?"

"I'm not bossy."

"No, of course not," he said.

"I'm not! None of my friends think so," I said.

"They're female."

"What, bossy is different to men than it is to women?"

"Women try to mother the guys they date," he said.

"Only when they act like children, which is three-quarters of the time."

"Maybe they act like children because women act like mothers."

"Is this a chicken-and-egg question? And what has it got to do with Wade? And why did you sniff a pair of boots?"

"They smell like childhood."

Just when I was getting good and riled, he had to say something like that. "They do, don't they?" I said. "They make me want to jump in mud puddles."

"It's hard to imagine you doing anything like that."

"Why?" I asked.

"You're always so neatly dressed."

"I have to be. It wouldn't be good for business if I showed up in ill-fitting, unflattering clothes." I'd thrown out all my comfort-grubbies when I'd moved up here, resolving to start my new life with a new look.

"I'd like to see you rumpled."

"It's not a pretty picture."

He looked as though he was going to say something, then his eyes shifted to the boots in my arms. "Are those okay, then?"

"Yes."

"Let's find the bike gear and get out of here."

Nine

Synthetic Fur

"I'm short, I know that," Elroy the wrestler said, "and the professionals are getting bigger and bigger, but it's personality that matters. It's character."

"Mmm-hmm," I murmured, noncommittal, more interested in a tooth that was feeling funny. I'd been clenching my jaw lately when feeling stressed, and was worried I might be damaging my teeth. I could ask Scott about it, of course, but then he'd probably want to look in my mouth, and he'd see all sorts of problems that needed fixing, and I'd end up having root canals and crowns and teeth pulled and drilling, and, and...

Elroy was sitting on the futon in my living room. The check he'd given me for his last costume had bounced, and he had managed to persuade me on the phone to let him come over and pay me for those pants and a new pair through a combination of barter and cash.

Wrestling at the local level paid next to nothing—maybe twenty dollars a night. Elroy made his living as a bouncer at a strip club, using his bulked-up muscles and wrestling-ring sneers to visually intimidate drunks.

He also made the odd dollar as a psychic, and it was that "skill" he was going to use to pay me.

"People like an underdog. They like the small guy who fights like a pit bull. They like to see the giants fall. Makes them feel strong, like they can fight anyone who tries to push them down."

"I can see that." I guess. I really couldn't understand why guys would watch wrestling. Women, sure: it was a chance to leer at near-naked men.

"So that's why I'm the Bulldog. Short, heavy and powerful."

I raised my brows and nodded, as if enlightened. Elroy had wavy, bleached-blond hair down to his shoulders, and a complexion like a permanent sunburn. The costume I had made him was a studded black leather collar, and a pair of loose synthetic fur pants in a tawny color, with a little stub of a tail over his butt. I thought it looked like a joke, but it was what he wanted.

"But do you have to do that leg-lifting bit, as if you're peeing on your opponent?" I asked. It was a move he'd made his trademark, and the young boys in the audience thought it hilarious.

"It's symbolic. You know. Metaphorical."

I felt vaguely insulted that my costume was forced to engage in such behavior, and was thankful the matches were considered family entertainment. Otherwise, Elroy might have asked me to attach a red doggie weenie to the pants, with one of those squeeze reservoirs like a squirting flower. He had that much class.

Still, he was basically a good guy, honest and enthusiastic. It was impossible to wish him anything but success with his underdog scheme.

"I've got an appointment in an hour," I said. "Shouldn't we get started?"

"Oh, okay. Can we close the curtains?"

I got up and pulled the thin, pale green curtains across the windows. The light was barely dimmed, but it did lend a more private, calming atmosphere to the room. It crossed my mind that I didn't actually know Elroy that well: he wasn't going to try something funny, was he? I wouldn't stand a chance in a fight against him.

"Got a candle?"

I took one off the bookshelf and put it on the coffee table, and lit it. "That all right?"

"Yeah. Now come sit beside me."

I gingerly sat at the other end of the futon.

He rubbed his palms quickly over his thighs, then pressed his palms together and closed his eyes, breathing deeply. Seconds ticked by.

His eyes opened, and he looked at me. "Give me your hands."

He looked as though he was taking himself seriously, which was reassuring. If he intended to pull something, he was a better actor than he showed in the ring. I gave him my hands.

"What is it you want to know?" he asked.

I gave a nervous laugh. "Oh, you know. The usual. Romance, work."

He squeezed my fingers, closing his eyes again. "There are men around you. They are attracted to you. Only one of them is right for you."

"Which one is he?"

"I can't say."

"Am I involved with him?" I asked.

"He's near, very near."

"How near?" I asked, suspicious.

"Very."

Gee, that was helpful. "What else about him?"

"He's fit, and near you in age. He thinks you're beautiful." Elroy opened his eyes, and the look in them was a little too intimate for my liking. "He will treat you well. You may think he is all wrong for you, but he's the right one."

"What's keeping me from seeing he is the one?" I asked. Elroy wasn't talking about himself, was he?

"The opinions of others. Or, what you think others will say. You have to follow your heart, not your head."

I'd be embarrassed to death to be seen on the arm of Elroy. He had to be talking about himself—there was no one else I knew I would be embarrassed to be seen with. I began to feel gyped. Psychic talents, my ass.

"What about my business?" I asked. Maybe he'd come up with something useful.

He closed his eyes again. "It will continue to grow. Maybe too much. Something will happen to make you balance your life when the work starts to be too much."

"I need all the work I can get." What was this, platitudes time? His prediction could apply to anyone.

Suddenly he squeezed my fingers, hard, and opened his eyes. "Wow. I just got a flash."

"Of what?"

He shook his head. "That's only happened two or three times before."

"What was it?"

"Something bad."

"Oh, great!"

"No, don't worry. It's bad, but it will be okay. It's part of the process, you know. The learning. You never learn when things are happy all the time."

It occurred to me that Elroy and Cassie might make a good pair.

"You'll begin to see more clearly after it happens," he said.

"Wonderful."

"Are you busy Saturday?"

I pulled my hands out of his. "Sorry. Gotta work."

Ten

Tighty Whities

I moved my playing piece halfway around the backgammon board, then looked at Wade from beneath my brow, smiling wickedly.

"What?"

"I was just thinking what my friends will say, when I tell them that my date involved owl vomit."

"I thought you were interested," he said.

Good Lord, the boy needed reassurance at every turn. "I was. It was fascinating, all those little bones and teeth stuck in a hair ball. It's just an unusual thing to do on a date, go slogging around in boots and examining vomit."

"But you enjoyed it? You didn't get too cold?"

I had gotten cold, I'd gotten much colder and wetter than I'd let on, but telling him would make him run into a dark corner and hide. Even now, sitting on the floor in his small apartment, I could feel the dampness of my pants clammy against my skin. The boots had been as waterproof as promised, but nothing could stop the blowing rain from hitting my legs.

"It was great."

It was a minor miracle I'd gotten him to take me back to his place. He seemed both pleased and wary to have me here.

Silence stretched. His dog, Mooch, stinking of wet fur, stretched and sighed where he lay a few feet away. We both looked at him, grateful for the distraction.

"Your turn," I said.

This was Date No. 5 with Mr. Wildlife, and still I hadn't gotten so much as a kiss. I'd taken his arm while we were at the zoo—Date No. 4—in way of encouragement, but it hadn't seemed to make an impression. I'd felt as if he wondered what was wrong with me, that I couldn't walk on my own.

And he didn't make so much as a vague allusion toward sex, not even when we'd been standing outside the elephant enclosure and seen wagging around the most monstrous penis to roam dry land. It had been huge, like a fifth leg, frightening enough in its immensity to invite at the very least a meeting of the eyes and silent exchange of awe. Of horror. Of amusement.

Anything.

How could you let a sight like that swing by without comment?

Of course, I couldn't.

"Bet the females run for their lives when they see that coming," I'd said.

He'd stared at me, and I'd felt my face go hot. I felt about as classy as a topless dancer.

"The penis of an elephant is capable of independent movement," he said just when I was ready to excuse myself and go hide in a rest room. "It has muscles so the male elephant, the bull, can find the vagina."

"Eww," I said, utterly revolted. I didn't want to think of elephant penises moving of their own volition, like thick pythons, slithering their way inside a female.

"And the cow's clitoris can reach sixteen inches in length, and become erect."

"I'll bet men wish human women were the same—it would save them a lot of trouble."

He gave me a faintly puzzled look, then laughed. It sounded forced.

"You must have learned a lot of strange things about animals in school," I said, feeling again as though I'd shown my tackiness.

"Sexual organs in the animal kingdom have a remarkably wide variety. The opossum, for example, has a forked penis—"

"Don't tell me! Ugh." The conversation had done absolutely nothing for my arousal level.

Now I looked at Wade across the coffee table upon which we were playing backgammon. Was he so shy that he needed me to make the moves? He seemed to like me well enough. He kept asking me out. What was the deal?

Enough of this dinking—or not dinking—around.

I crawled on all fours around the coffee table, moving slowly, staring into Wade's eyes as if I were a stalking cat.

His eyes widened, and he leaned away as I approached.

I stopped only when my face was inches from his own, still staring at him. He blinked, eyelids fluttering. I closed the last few inches separating us, and lay my lips against his own.

He didn't move away, so I kept my lips there, then moved them against his own, and with the tip of my tongue lightly painted his lower lip.

And then, finally, his hand came up and he brushed his fingers into my hair. I could feel him shaking.

He leaned forward, so that I was forced back onto my knees. He put his arms around me and deepened the kiss.

Victory!

I was too caught up in the mechanics of the kiss to feel any sparks. It was my usual problem: stuck in my head, unable to let loose. But really, I had to keep my senses in this case, anyway. One false move and he would retreat. It was more important that he gain some confidence, than that I get my kicks.

Wasn't it?

He was a wet kisser, and I tried to not think of some large animal slobbering all over my lips and chin.

I put my hands on either side of his face and gently held him back, retaking control of the kiss and dotting his lips and skin with closemouthed, dry kisses. Then, when he was properly still, I moved down the side of his neck, pulling at the neck of his sweatshirt with my index finger to expose an inch more of skin on which to suck.

His hands fluttered above my sides, landing uncertainly.

I pushed him back, forcing him to lie on the carpet. His head hit Mooch's rear foot, and the dog jerked awake, raising his head to look at us as if affronted.

Wade wasn't protesting, and I took his silence as an invitation to continue. I slid my hand under his sweatshirt, discovering a T-shirt underneath. I yanked it out of his pants, then slid my hand up his bare belly toward his chest.

His skin was cool, and soft with flab. Fully clothed, I hadn't seen how out of shape he was. I pushed his shirts up past his downy-haired nipples and ran my hands over his collar bone: it was as delicately built as a chicken wing. I squeezed his shoulders, and my fingers sank into cool, doughlike flesh.

Where was my manly man, my Mr. Wilderness? All I had before me was an elongated city marshmallow.

Still, he was a nice guy, and I was certain there had to be a wild animal under there somewhere. I bent and kissed his chest, and trailed kisses down toward his belly button. I sent a scouting fingertip into it, checking for debris, and was glad I had when I found the hardened clump of lint and dead skin.

Why did men never clean their navels? Why?

In any case, my tongue wasn't going in there, that was for sure. And it seemed rude to dig out the crud and flick it aside. I moved on, kissing the side of his soft belly while my hands went to work on the fastenings of his pants.

I got the button and zipper undone, then looked up at him as I parted the fabric. He had his eyes closed, and was lying still as a virgin.

Which brought an unwelcome idea to mind.

He wasn't one, was he? At thirty-six? Surely it wasn't possible. I'd known a few quiet, nondescript guys, and most of them were raging sexual beasts beneath the placid exterior. They might not have women falling all over them, but once they had one in their clutches, they went nuts, showing a hell of a lot more innovation and attentive enthusiasm than good-looking guys who didn't have to work for their pleasures.

Wade was a decent-looking, friendly guy. I couldn't believe that at least one woman hadn't let him have his way with her.

He was wearing Jockey shorts, and his penis was nowhere in sight. I opened the fly of his pants wider, then yanked on them until Wade obligingly raised his hips so I could slide them down.

Ah, there it was. A small bulge nestled alongside his testicles. It didn't look particularly excited to meet me.

I lay my hand over the white cotton and pressed, rubbing gently, waiting to feel a change in size.

Nothing. It remained the size of a garden slug.

I waited a little longer, massaging, bending to breathe on it through the knit as if giving it the breath of life. There was a bit of stirring, not as much as there should be, but something.

Hoping he'd have told me if there was anything communicable down there I wouldn't want to touch, I slipped my hand under the band of his briefs and touched the frightened creature skin-to-skin.

I compressed the entirety of it within the palm of my hand. I teased the head with my fingertip, feeling the opening at the top, looking for that first telltale drop of pre-cum. I cupped and tickled his balls. There was a slight thickening, and nothing more.

Maybe he was just nervous. Maybe he was one of those guys who trained himself to not get hard, so that he wouldn't come too soon.

I lay down on my side, my head level with his chest, and continued to play.

"Hannah," he said, his voice cracking.

I cradled his penis like a baby mouse in my hand. "Yes?" I answered, practicing in my head the reassurances I would give. *It's okay, it happens to everyone sometimes. No, I don't mind. Don't worry about it. I'm enjoying just touching you. Relax.*

"There's something you should know."

My hand stilled. Oh, God. He *did* have an STD.

He took a shaky breath. "This is my first time—"

He really *was* a virgin? What did one do with a virgin? I was going to have to be even more reassuring than I had been already. "It is? How far have you gone with a woman?" I asked, trying to sound nonchalant.

He made a gurgling sound, something like a hysterical laugh in the back of his throat. "With a woman? A kiss, is all."

I frowned, sitting up and looking at him, hand still on his privates. He glanced at me, then went back to staring at the ceiling. His emphasis on "with a woman" struck me as odd. "So no one has ever touched you like I've been doing?" I asked, to clarify, wanting to take my hand out of his underpants but not wanting to make the guy feel rejected, in case my suspicion was wrong.

"This is my first time being…intimate…with a woman. It's been men up till now."

I snatched my hand out of his shorts, wanting to bolt to the sink and scrub it with bleach and hot water at the thought of where his penis had ventured.

"Don't worry, I don't have HIV or anything," he said

sarcastically, and pushed himself into a sitting position, finally looking me in the eye.

"Why?" I asked hoarsely, as the information sank in and I realized I'd been throwing myself at a gay guy. Beyond the embarrassment of my idiocy for not figuring it out on my own was a feeling of being utterly unfeminine. There must be something masculine about me, if a gay guy would go for me. I wanted to cry. "Why did you answer my ad?"

"It's a new city, a new job. I wanted to try a new life," he said, the previous sarcasm giving way to a sad resignation.

I wanted to hit him. Of course he couldn't alter his sexual orientation on a whim—and he a biologist! He should know better! And he'd been selfish enough to drag me into his experiment.

"I've always thought women were beautiful," he said, "so I thought I might give it a try. I wanted to see what it was like to live like everyone else."

"Oh lucky me, to be your test rat," I said. I was in no mood to be sympathetic.

"I really like you. You're smart and confident. I wish it would have worked." He glanced down at his crotch. "It just didn't."

"But why me?" I asked. I didn't care what he was going through, I was too busy trying to find sense in a dating world suddenly gone upside down and inside out. "Do I come across as masculine?" I whined.

"I don't know why you." He shrugged, and gave his unresponsive weenie a quick rub. "I just liked you. It sounded like we'd have fun together. We did have fun together, didn't we?"

"I guess." If you call it that. I tramped through the rain and looked at owl vomit for this?

"I mean, we can still be friends, can't we? I'm sorry if I hurt you, but it's really not about you. I'd like to still do things with you."

My lips parted, and I stared in incredulity. I was getting the same speech I'd given guys in the past. And it *was* about me—he'd chosen me, after all—and no, I didn't want to be his friend. I suddenly realized that the only thing that had kept me interested this long was the challenge of overcoming his passivity.

Without that challenge, he was just a boring, confused guy with a nice dog.

And he'd let me fondle his weenie. Thank God I hadn't put it in my mouth. The thought of where it had been made me ill.

I stood up and found my coat, feeling a thousand miles from my own movements. "I've gotta think about this," I lied. "I'll let you know."

"You aren't mad at me, are you?"

"Surprised, is all. I'll let you know, okay?" I said, incapable of more. I had to get out of there.

"Okay. Call me."

Yeah, right.

Eleven

Walking Shoes

"At least you know now why he was so unsure all the time," Louise said as we crossed the street from my house to Laurelhurst Park, beginning our Sunday constitutional. The park was wooded with fir at this end, where we poor folk lived. Half a block away on either side, the houses lining the edge of the park were big, old and expensive, with carefully tended yards.

"Yeah, he had no clue how he was supposed to behave as a heterosexual. I suppose I should think it funny, how worried he must have been the whole time, that he'd give himself away," I said, still not thinking it funny. "And no wonder he gave me such a strange look when I made that comment about the elephant clitoris making things easy on a guy. He had no idea what I was talking about."

"Are you still upset about it?" she asked. "I mean, are you okay with it? That had to be a blow to your ego."

"I worked out my own form of therapy," I said, smiling.

"How's that?" she asked, curious.

"I made a Voodoo Wade doll."

"What?"

"Voodoo Wade," I repeated. "I made a little doll and dressed it like him, and then I hung it by a length of filament in front of the window in my sewing room. He spins in the drafts, sort of like a twisting corpse on a noose."

"And this helps?"

"Well, then I was downtown and got the bright idea to stop in a toy store and look for a slingshot. I couldn't find one, but I *did* find a fabulous rubber band gun."

"Don't tell me."

"Yup. So whenever I start feeling cranky about Wade's sexual orientation experiment, I sit on the floor with my gun and shoot him."

"I love it."

"It's very therapeutic. I do his screams myself, which Cassie finds a bit disturbing. I have to do it quietly at night, or she gets upset."

We took one of the paved paths that wound through the interior, past lawns of sloping green.

"Are you going to give up on the Internet dating now?" she asked, sounding a bit like a scolding mother. It was hard to take someone with freckles and curls seriously, though.

"I don't know. I mean, it wasn't a dangerous experience. It was just weird." I wasn't willing yet to admit my mate-shopping plan was a failure. "You haven't had any offers to meet anyone?" I asked.

"I haven't been replying to any of my e-mails," she said quietly.

"Louise!" What was wrong with my friends?

"It doesn't seem fair."

"Fair to whom?"

"To them. Not when I'm not really interested. You're going to give me a lecture about this, I know, but, well, I'm kind of interested in Derek."

"The divorced guy? Oh, Louise. Say it isn't so."

"I know, I know. I know all about guys on the rebound, divorce, all of that. But he's so easy to talk to, and we went to dinner again on Friday—"

"Louise!"

"I know! I'm bad. But it was just friendly, I promise."

"You _know_ this isn't a good idea."

"I know," she said.

"But you're going to do it anyway."

"It's just friendly."

We came out the other end of the park and crossed the street to the opposite sidewalk, heading deeper into the Laurelhurst neighborhood. I liked to imagine which house I would live in, if I had the money.

"Does he show any interest in you, beyond the friendly?" I asked.

"I don't know. I can't tell," she said, warming to the topic, probably taking my question for a sign I thought it was okay, after all. "Sometimes I think so, but all the guys who work there, they're counselors so they're a little like women in some ways. They all like to talk, and I mean about people, not sports or toys. It's not like your average computer or business guy. So I don't know if he's opening up to me more than he would to anyone else."

"Who suggested dinner?"

"It was mutual. Or maybe he did. It just kind of happened. We got off at the same time, and as we were walking out we started talking about that new Chinese restaurant a block away, and we decided to try it." She peeked at me. "What do you think?"

"I don't know," I said, and I didn't know. Who's to say it might not work? If it wasn't going to, she'd find out soon enough on her own, and then I could say, "I told you so." "Be careful," I added.

"I know!"

"Maybe you should meet a few of those guys who wrote to you. It'll keep you from getting too caught up in Derek."

"Yeah, maybe," she said.

I knew she wouldn't. "Cassie hasn't gone out with anyone, either," I admitted. My friends were a bunch of cowards. "Do you know if Scott has?"

"He did, last night," she said, and cast me a glance.

"You're kidding!"

"Some woman who just got her law degree, and has started working at the Clackamas County D.A.'s office. He says she's really smart."

"Really." My surprise was being replaced by some other, vaguely uncomfortable feeling. She had a law degree. Huh. "Is she pretty?"

"He says so. She's almost as tall as he is. He says it's nice to be able to look a woman in the eye for a change."

I only came up to his chin. Not that it mattered. "Does he like her?"

"He says it's too soon to tell yet. You'll have to call

him, and get the full story. We got interrupted when his beeper went off.''

"Hmm.'' The news brought me down for some reason. "Yeah, I'll have to call him.''

I get a confused gay guy, and Scott finds a beautiful lawyer. I should have been happy for him. Instead, I was jealous, and I thought I knew why. The Internet dating was my idea: I deserved to find success first.

I hoped the lawyer thing fizzled. She was probably too pushy for him, anyway. Too aggressive. I didn't have to worry.

Twelve

Embroidered Linen

"How do I get rid of that little picture?"

"It's the PIP button, Dad. It means 'picture in picture,'" I said as Dad fiddled with the remote control, trying to remove the box in the lower right-hand corner of the television screen.

The sound went mute, then came back on at wall-shaking volume.

"Here, I'll do it!" I said, grabbing the remote and returning all to rights.

"I don't know why they have to make it so complicated. What are all these buttons for, anyway? 'Learning.' What's a 'learning' button do?"

"You point the remote at your skull, press it, and suddenly it all makes sense."

"Ha, ha, very funny."

I got up and went to go help Mom in the kitchen. There was a pork roast in the oven, seasoned with rosemary, and the smell was making my mouth water. Apples were waiting to be peeled and diced for applesauce, so I took a knife and set to work as Mom started cutting shortening into flour for biscuits.

Home was a two-storied 1930 farmhouse, in a neighborhood of houses of much newer vintage. There was nothing left of the original farm, the land having been developed long before my parents bought the house. Mom had liked the old look of it, and Dad had spent every year since making repairs to the structure, and swearing that, "Next time we're buying a new house." The threat used to scare me, thinking we'd have to move, but eventually I got used to it and realized he had no intention of relocating.

The yards, both front and back, were filled with bird feeders and baths, and Mom's carefully tended beds of roses. There was a workshop out back that Dad had built, for his "projects," but mostly it seemed a place for him to store his junk, out of Mom's sight.

When Mom wasn't gardening or feeding Dad, she was volunteering at the library twice a week. She loved popular novels, and while Dad would sit and watch his games on the television, the volume loud enough to vibrate bones, she would be in her own world inside her head. I think all those years of teaching third-graders trained her to tune out at will.

All in all, I thought I was pretty lucky in the parents I'd gotten. They weren't sophisticated, they weren't wealthy, but they were kind and loving, and were still together, despite the occasional snippy argument that I was, thankfully, no longer around to hear.

"Have you been meeting any nice boys?" Mom asked.

"There's no one at the moment." I had told her about the unexpected end to my relationship with Wade.

"I just can't stop thinking about that biologist. That poor confused boy."

I frowned at her. "Poor confused boy? What about me? I'm the one you should feel sorry for."

She waved off my words. "You're strong, you always come through. But that poor boy. How miserable he must be. Are you going to stay in touch, stay his friend?"

"No! Jeez, Mom, why would I?"

"He sounds like he needs a friend."

"He shouldn't have lied to me. He should have let me know up front what was going on."

"Poor boy."

"I didn't do anything wrong!" She was making me feel guilty, when I was the victim. Wasn't I? "I don't want him as a friend. We really have very little in common."

"Then why did you date him? You should be friends with the men you date. The passion doesn't last, you know. You need a friendship for when it goes away."

"Do you feel like you and Dad have a friendship?"

She scooped biscuit batter and dropped it in rough mounds on a cookie sheet. "We have comfort, and familiarity."

"Mom?" Comfort and familiarity? That was all?

She smiled, rather sadly, I thought. "Choose someone you can talk to."

"You and Dad love each other, don't you?"

"Of course I love your father. He's just not much for conversation."

I added water and sugar to the pan of diced apples

and set them on the stove to cook, my rosy view of my parents shaken.

I didn't really want to know of the disappointments my mother had suffered in her marriage. I wanted to think it was happy and content, and that the same situation was waiting for me, once I found the right guy.

I especially didn't like to think that all that time Mom had been sitting with a Jackie Collins novel in her hands, she was secretly wishing Dad would shut off the television and talk to her. How long had Mom been yearning for something more than she had?

Were there any happy marriages, once you looked beyond the surface?

Maybe I'd be better off staying single, and childless.

But no, that didn't hold appeal, either. I could too easily see a future filled with day after day of endless alterations, thousands of pants to be hemmed, bridesmaids' dresses to be constructed, pillow shams to be made.

I could spend the next fifty years in a cramped apartment surrounded by other people's clothes, never advancing beyond subsistence level, never getting far enough ahead to buy a house or to take a real vacation. With age my fingers would cramp with arthritis, I'd lose my ability to sew, and then eventually I'd die, a forgotten old woman with no one to mourn her passing.

Ugh. How was that for a depressing thought? At least with a husband I'd have someone to carp at, and blame my troubles on.

I spread the hand-embroidered linen cloth on the table, set it, then wandered back out to the living room and dropped onto the couch. Dad had a golf tournament on, which was about the least offensive one could get, sound-wise, in televised sports. Even the announcers had hushed voices.

Dad and I sat in silence, watching soft-bellied men in saggy clothing.

"Hey, Dad."

"Unn?" he grunted, not taking his eyes from the screen.

"If you had to give me advice about what type of guy to marry, what would it be?"

"What?"

"Dad, hello?" I said, waving my arms.

He finally looked away from the screen. "I don't know."

"Come on, Dad, you must have at least one piece of wisdom to impart."

"I'm not good at this stuff."

I stared at him, not letting him look back at the screen, willing him to say more. He had lived a long time, worked with a lot of men. He should know a thing or two.

"Marry someone you enjoy spending time with."

"Doesn't it matter if he has a good job?"

Dad shrugged. "No. That's it, someone whose company you enjoy. I don't know what else to say."

I suppose it had a certain merit to it. After all, if you didn't enjoy spending time with someone, why would you marry him? But on the other hand, if you're in love, even with a loser who is going to bring you misery, you probably think you like the guy's company just fine. The good job would be some consolation, I'd think.

"Why do you think Mom fell for you?"

He blinked at me, and then his eyes lost their focus as he dug back through memory, his brows pulling together as he tried to find an answer.

''I don't really know,'' he said at last. ''I just got lucky, I guess.''

''Why did you fall for her?''

''She was about the prettiest, sweetest, smartest girl I'd ever met,'' he said, face softening.

He stared into space for another stretch of time, and then the frown returned. ''Why *did* she fall for me?''

Thirteen

Polyester Brocade with Garters

It had been a long day, and now I was stuck in traffic between Hillsboro and Beaverton, two of the suburbs known for gridlock hell. Cars rolled slowly along in neutral, and it took an average of three cycles of the lights to get through an intersection.

Since eight-thirty in the morning I had been burning unleaded from Vancouver to Wilsonville, from downtown to the city limits. It was one of those days where none of my clients lived or worked near any of the others, and today was the only day they could fit me into their schedules.

I had at least three thousand dollars' worth of clothes hanging from the rack across my back seat, pins marking where jacket sleeves had to be shortened, bodice darts put in, hems taken up; there were wool pants and a leather jacket in need of linings; one woman had given me a designer skirt suit and asked me to take jacket and skirt apart to make her a pair of pants. She liked the fabric. Someone else had given me a fragile 1920's black velvet opera cape to be copied.

All of it together would take me no more than a week

to do, including trips to the fabric store, and that allowed for procrastination, an activity I was becoming addicted to. As business flourished and I felt marginally more secure about the money situation, I was getting progressively more inclined to waste time. It was a bad habit that I would have to keep an eye on.

There was no work I could do at the moment, though, stuck in traffic. It was guilt-free daydreaming time. With my mind free, though, it went right to one of my teeth that was showing signs of becoming cold sensitive, and it made me wince when I ate chocolate. I worried that that might mean a cavity.

I tried to think of something else. I flipped to the 80's station on the radio, and howled along to Cyndi Lauper's "Girls Just Want to Have Fun," although my heart wasn't really in it.

Fun. I wasn't getting much of that, was I? Since the Wade fiasco, I hadn't had a date. I had been leery of the Internet for a few days, not checking my personals mailbox, and then when I finally did there were several nasty notes from guys who were pissed that I hadn't written back. It had brought on a distaste for the entire system, and I hadn't checked my mail since.

Traffic oozed forward. The late-afternoon sun began heading for the Coast Range, and shadows from the tall Douglas firs leaned across the road. Headlights were turned on against the falling dusk.

I was horny, I was lonely for a man, and there was no solution in sight. No fun for this girl.

Or was there?

Rising out of the murky gloom up ahead was a phallus-shaped tower, outlined in tiny white Christmas tree lights. An illuminated sign beneath it read, The Purple Palace, and in smaller, capitalized letters, Adult Superstore.

The traffic gave me plenty of time to contemplate as I approached the entrance to the parking lot. I'd never been in such a place, and imagined it was mostly middle-aged men who frequented them. I pictured private movie booths in back, complete with tissue dispenser and vinyl seats, a bulletin board with the names and numbers of escort services and rack upon rack of pornographic magazines.

But I also imagined they'd have vibrators and dildos.

I'd had a vibrator once, ordered from a catalog that catered to women, but it had died on me. I still had it, being paranoid that the day I tossed it in the trash would be the day the garbage can would fall over and the pink thing would roll out into the middle of the street, just as some kids were riding by on their bicycles, and they'd pick it up and ask what it was. Or worse yet, a cute male jogger would come by, and already *know* what it was.

I wanted to order another, but every package that came to the door was met with curiosity by Cassie, and although she would likely have cheered me on for buying a vibrator, I couldn't bear the idea of her knowing about it. I didn't want to discuss my masturbation habits with my housemate.

The parking lot was nearly empty. The few windows were papered over from the inside. The building was new, and could have passed for an electronics store— or, given the turreted tower up top, a kid's pizza parlor.

My heart thumped in my chest as the turnoff came nearer. Was I really going to do this?

I flipped on my blinker and turned, and told myself that a browse inside would get me off the road and allow the traffic a chance to thin out. And if I didn't buy anything, I could entertain my friends telling them about my visit.

The door had a warning posted that one must be twenty-one to enter. I clutched my purse, wondering if they would card me.

I pushed the door open, and was greeted by glaring white. Fluorescent lighting reflected off white walls and white tile flooring with a brilliance that put Target and K mart to shame. A heavyset woman sat in the center of a round cashier's island, reading a book. She looked up at my entry, and smiled a greeting.

"Hello."

"Hello," I said back.

Why did she have to acknowledge me? She should know better. She should let customers slink and dart in the shadows.

"If there's anything I can help you with, let me know."

"Okay. Thanks."

I slunk down the first open aisle. What could I possibly ask her? "Excuse me, but could you recommend a good vibrator? I'd like a moderate amount of flexibility, variable speeds, and above all, reliability. I'm going to put it to hard use, and don't want it breaking down on me. Ability to stimulate the G-spot? Why, yes, that would be nice."

The aisle I'd chosen catered to the bondage artist in

all of us. Straps and cuffs and rings of leather, metal, polyester webbing, and fake leopard fur hung from the Peg-Board walls. I paused in front of a set of large clear suction cups with rings, meant for use in the shower or bath. They looked like something Spiderman might use.

If Louise or Cassie were here, we'd have a good giggle. But just on my own... I imagined being fastened, spread-eagle in a large tub while an anonymous man poured warm water over my groin. Ohhhh...

I scampered out of that aisle, and found myself in videos, in the section devoted to gay men. I picked up a cover at random: *Wild Men of the Forest.* The actors were covered in thick body hair. Why hadn't Wade looked like that? But he'd probably enjoy the video more than I.

Sitting on top of the rack was a lavender plush penis, two feet long, like something you'd win at a carnival. Sitting next to it was an enormous pair of green plush breasts, with a strap attached to wear them over your neck.

I smiled, beginning to relax a bit. The Purple Palace had a sense of humor.

I wandered, and then heard voices. I looked up, and saw a couple in their mid-twenties examining lubricants.

Two women my own age were going through the racks of lewd greeting cards. Another young couple was looking at lingerie. There were no men here alone. There were no older people.

Nothing was as I had expected. Everyone looked like me, only less furtive. There was no reason to be embarrassed, but still I could not shake the urge to skulk.

I felt too exposed shopping for my sexual pleasure in public.

I made myself go to the vibrator section, my steps slowing at the sight of toys meant for boys. There was a battery-operated, latex mouth lined with rubbery stubs like hundreds of teeth. I couldn't imagine any guy having the guts to put his winkie in that. There was a vulva, complete with synthetic curls of hair. Just a vulva. No thighs, no lower belly, no butt. It looked as though it had been cut off a cadaver.

Did guys see dildos the same way?

I moved on. There were plastic beads on a string, for sticking up one's butt, there was a vibrating finger—how lazy did you have to be to buy that?—a hand that looked as if it had come off a mannequin, and there were dildos.

Dildos the size of which I had never seen, and could imagine no earthly use for, unless one wanted to keep one by the door to use on intruders. The sight of a woman confidently holding one of those monsters in her hands would be enough to scare any man away. And if it didn't, a smack on the side of the head with it and he'd be out.

I could see the headline: Woman Subdues Attacker With Giant Dildo! And the article itself. "Police agree that silicone dildos make better defensive weapons than handguns. Their flexibility is reminiscent of a rubber hose, and leaves no mark except a red welt in the shape of the penis head. Being attacked by a giant dildo has become known on the street as being 'weenie whipped.'"

I was almost tempted to buy one of the monsters, but

the one I liked—it had grotesque, finger-thick veining up its sides—was eighty-five dollars. Pity.

There was no one in the vibrator area, and I made my choice as quickly as I could, getting momentarily stuck over which diameter to buy. Too small, and what was the point? Too big, and it would be uncomfortable. I ended up with one of the bent ones meant for hitting the G-spot, gladly passing by the pink ones with the little latex animals squatting at the base, their tongues sticking out to lick your clitoris as you got off.

Boxed vibrator in hand, the clear side turned toward my body so no one could see it, I headed toward the cashier. The woman was still there, but was ringing up the purchases of one of the couples. I decided to wait until they were gone, and dawdled in the lingerie section.

There was an assortment of cheap corsets that caught my eye, some of them almost pretty, made of white brocade with a ruffle around the top edge. They were even more expensive than the giant dildo. I examined their construction, deciding I could make one myself without too much trouble, assuming I would ever have occasion to wear such a thing.

I looked up at the cash register, and the couple was gone. And so was the female clerk. A pimply-faced guy who couldn't be more than twenty-two was sitting behind the counter, scratching at his erupting skin.

Oh, jeez. It was just like the grocery store. I always ended up buying a box of tampons when the only cashier available was a teenage boy, with his snickering friend doing the bagging.

This was a sex shop. The guy's job was to ring up

sex toys and videos. There should be no embarrassment here, no sniggering, no smirking. I made myself walk up to the counter and put down the box, cellophane-side up.

"Find what you were looking for?" the guy asked, pulling it toward him.

"Uh-huh."

He turned the box over. "We just got this model in. Haven't gotten any feedback on it yet, but it's a good company."

Why didn't he shut up? Shut up!

He pulled a basket out from beneath the counter, full of batteries of various sizes. "Still, we have to test the things before we let them out the door. Sometimes they're faulty."

I stared in horror as he opened up the box and with his bare, pimple-picking hands took out my vibrator and twisted it open at the base. He slid in two AA batteries.

A couple came to stand in line behind me.

The clerk twisted the base back on and turned the speed adjuster. It clicked through low, medium, and high, and nothing happened. He turned it over in his hands, shook it, then squinted at the white plastic thing as it pointed back at him with its shape like a bent finger.

"Should I go get another off the shelf?" I asked, the words squeezed out of my throat.

"No, wait a minute." He opened the base again, peered in at the batteries and at the lid, then dumped one battery out and reversed its direction. This time it worked, and the vibrator hummed to life.

"There we go. It's a quiet one, isn't it? Good company," he said.

"Kkkk," I said, a noise meant to be affirmative. I wanted to shove it down his throat. It sounded like an unmuffled motorcycle to my ears. I could feel the couple behind me watching with interest.

I got out my money as the clerk took the batteries out and returned the vibrator to its box. I was going to have to boil the thing, to get his germs off it.

"You want to be on our mailing list?" he asked as I paid.

"No!" I said. I grabbed my bag and scooted for the door, avoiding the eyes of the couple.

I shoved through the door and out into the brightly lit parking lot. A very brightly lit parking lot, and crowded with chanting people.

Picketers.

Twenty or so women were marching in a circle, carrying signs:

No Sex Shops Near Our Schools!

Protect Our Children!

Do You Want This In *Your* Neighborhood?

Kids + Porn – Bad Idea!

The bright lights were from the news vans. Oh, God. I felt faint.

I tried to sneak by the protesters, most of whom looked like soccer moms, the type whose lives revolved obsessively around their kids. They came to within six feet of my car, sitting there with Hannah's Custom Sewing painted on the door, along with my cell phone number.

I was almost there when a light shone in my eyes and a woman in a Gore-Tex jacket with the logo of a local news station on one breast stepped in front of me, holding a microphone.

"As a patron of The Purple Palace, what do you think of its being located so near to a grade school?" she asked.

"A patron?" I asked, in an effort at denial.

Her eyes went to the bag I clutched in my hands.

"Do you feel that this store is a danger to children?" she asked.

I looked helplessly around. "Children?"

"There is a school four blocks from here. Isn't The Purple Palace a danger to them? Doesn't it encourage the presence of sexual predators?"

"I don't think I saw any predators in there," I said, fumbling for my key, trying to stay in front of my name on the car door.

"Kids walk by here every day on their way to and from school."

"Yes?" I said, finally fitting my key into the lock, not able to concentrate.

"So that doesn't concern you?"

"It's not like they'd be allowed in," I said, feeling a little braver now that freedom was almost at hand. I opened the car door. "I'll bet the kids see more porn from their dads' stashes than they ever will from this place."

I dived in my car and slammed the door.

That vibrator had better be worth it.

Fourteen

White Satin

"Can I use your iron?" Cassie asked, standing in the doorway to my sewing room, her white work shirt over her arm.

"Of course." I had a professional steam iron, and a sturdy ironing board that never came down. I appreciated that she asked; once she hadn't, and had somehow managed to get sticky gray gunk on the surface of the iron. The gunk had transferred to a client's silk dress the next time I used it.

"Are you making a wedding dress?"

I was on the floor, yards of white satin covering a wide swathe of the room. I was laying thin paper pattern pieces out over it.

"Yeah. It's this woman's third wedding, if you can believe it. How do some women get so lucky?"

"You call that lucky, being divorced twice?" Cassie asked, spreading her shirt on the board.

"I mean, lucky to have found three guys who want to marry you."

"But what type of guys?"

"You take the fun out of things," I complained.

"I'm keeping you rooted in reality."

A funny thing to hear, coming from her. "How's this for unreality. She says her younger sister had a wedding dress made and booked a reception site while she was still single. And somehow a guy appeared and they fell in love and got married in time to use the reservation. Can you believe it?"

The iron huffed steam into the collar of her shirt. "She was ready, and she knew it."

"But to have the dress made! And put a deposit down on a site!"

"It's like I've been saying. When you're ready, the right person will appear."

"I wish I'd hurry up and get ready," I grumbled.

"The more you want it, the farther from it you will be."

"That makes no sense."

She shrugged, finishing up on her shirt.

"Do you have any prospects, yourself?" I asked.

A hint of a smile teased her lips.

"Cass! Tell!"

"You wouldn't like him. He works at the pub with me."

"Why wouldn't I like him?"

"He has long hair. And he's younger."

"How much younger?" I asked.

"He's twenty-four."

I curled my lip. "Twenty-four? Yuck. What do you want with a guy eight years younger than you? Jeez, it's bad enough when they're our own age. At twenty-four, they're practically still teenagers."

"I knew you'd say something like that."

I made a show of biting my lip. "Sorry. There must be something good about him, if you like him. Twenty-four, they're still near their sexual peak at that age."

"I know," she said, smiling.

"So what else does he do, except work at the pub?"

"He's a musician, and writes songs."

I tried to keep my face serene and open.

"He's also in grad school at P.S.U., to be a teacher."

"Oh. That sounds okay."

She gave me a look, and I tried to appear innocent. She thought I put too much emphasis on a man's professional goals. She'd be happy staying in a tiny place like this rented house, listening to an occasionally employed lover strum out his songs on the guitar well into the future.

As usual, I didn't know if she was the crazy one, or I was.

"If it turns into something, you'll bring him home, won't you?" I asked. "We can have dinner or something."

"Of course, Mother."

"What's his name?" I asked as she was leaving.

"Jack."

Jack, the twenty-four-year-old student and musician. Well, as long as she was happy.

I went back to work on the dress, pinning the pattern pieces into place and then cutting them out, double and triple checking that I had everything laid out right. The heavy silk satin was thirty-two dollars a yard on sale, and I didn't want to make a mistake.

The story about the girl who'd had the dress made and reserved the reception site preyed on my mind. Was it so obvious when one was ready? Was it so instinctive? And if it was, why wasn't I as naturally aware of not being ready to meet my soul mate?

I felt past ready.

Maybe Cassie was wrong. Maybe it wasn't a matter of being ready and the person coming to you. Maybe it was a matter of making things happen, and sending out the vibe that if you were confident all would occur as you wished.

With a dress and a site waiting, that girl must have been one determined chick.

I put down my scissors and crawled over to the rickety bookcase against one wall, where my pile of inch-thick bridal magazines were stashed.

In all those pages there were maybe six or seven wedding dresses that I liked, and none that I would wear exactly as they were. I flipped the magazines open to the marked places, examining the gowns. I liked the high-waisted element of one, the lace-over-lining of another, the split sleeves of a third. And there was a pair of off-white shoes covered in Baroque beadwork that begged to be made.

If you sew it, he will come.

The thought drifted through my mind like a whisper from the gods.

If it worked for Kevin Costner and baseball players, why not for me, and a fiancé?

And it was a mentally healthy thing to do. Sometimes I thought the only reason I wanted to get married was to get the dress. This would take away that desire, and leave me free to pursue marriage for all the right reasons.

It would save me a lot of time, too, when I had to plan my wedding. With the dress taken care of, I would be free to concentrate on flower arrangements and catering.

I grabbed pen and paper, and began sketching out my dream gown.

It was an eminently sane thing to do.

Fifteen

Nasty Sweater

"She'd had this bit of popcorn shell wedged beneath her gum for at least a month," Scott said. "The tissue was inflamed, there was pus and blood oozing out—"

"For God's sake, stop it!"

"You really should get a cleaning and a checkup."

"When I can afford it," I said, tearing off a piece of cinnamon roll, my pinkie raised as if that could save the other fingers from getting coated in syrup.

We were sitting on stools at one of the tiny tables in a bakery at Pioneer Place, the shopping center in the center of downtown. Scott had a couple hours free, and had asked me to go clothes shopping with him. He claimed to be helpless in the men's department, and in need of my expertise.

Not that he always took my advice. In one of the bags at our feet was a sweater in an atrocious mix of earth tones, squiggled together like the matting of threads on my sewing room floor.

"I'll give you a discount," he said.

"I don't want you looking in my mouth."

"Then Neena. She can do it."

"I'll think about it," I said. I'd met Scott's dental practice partner, a petite Indian woman, once, and I'd liked her. She had a soft voice and a calm air, although she also, according to Scott, had an enthusiasm for doing work that was not absolutely necessary. It was perfectionism that led her to it, not greed.

I, however, did not want anyone messing around in my mouth at all, much less more than they had to. I still had the cold-sensitive tooth, but was doing a good job of persuading myself I didn't need to do anything about it. There was no reason to invite visitors with sharp metal tools.

"So what's going on with you and this prosecutor woman?" I asked to change the subject. "Louise said you'd been out three or four times."

"Twice."

"And?"

"And what? She's smart, and seems interesting, but I don't really know her yet," he said.

"But you're going to see her again?"

"Yeah, why not?"

"You don't sound too enthusiastic," I said.

"I don't know. It could work out. I'm just not sure yet."

"We always know, though, don't we? Even from the beginning," I said.

"I don't."

"Sure you do. It's always the thing that you wondered about at first, the thing that made part of you doubt. It builds and builds until it tears the relationship apart, and you're left wondering why you just didn't listen to your gut in the first place."

"I don't think you can know that quickly. I think there's instant attraction, but it takes a long time to know if someone is a good match," he said.

"Maybe that's a difference between guys and women, then."

"Have you ever fallen for someone you weren't instantly attracted to?"

I squished cinnamon roll between my fingers, thinking back on my sorry dating history. "How many guys have I ever fallen for, period?" I said, meeting his eyes. "What, maybe two? I mean really fallen for, not just dated for a while. Two guys, in nearly fifteen years of dating. That's a sad record."

I was beginning to feel depressed. It had been less than a year since my last relationship had ended: did I have another six years to go before I was due my next allotment of love?

"Sounds about average to me."

"How many times have you been in love?" I asked.

"Three or four times. Not that it was always mutual."

"Aw. How could someone not love you back?"

"Beats me. They'd get free dental care for life. How could anyone pass that up?"

"And there's the manly car, too."

"Maybe I need to work a little harder on my package," he said.

"Your what?"

"My package. My act. The things I have to offer."

"For God's sake, Scott. There's nothing wrong with your 'package.' You're in shape, you're a good provider, you're clean and polite and don't have any bad habits except that obsession with Tater Tots. The lawyer chick wants you. What makes you think there's anything wrong with your 'package'?''

He looked into the remains of his coffee, and shrugged.

I snorted. ''And they say women are the insecure ones.''

Sixteen

Blue Uniform

"You like to fish?"

"Huh?" I said, turning away from the giant tank of salmon. A young guy with shoulders broad enough to sleep on was, unbelievably, talking to me.

"Do you like to fish?" he asked again.

"Oh. I haven't gone since I was little. I like watching them, though. They're pretty, all silvery and undulating," I said, stretching out the word, unnnn-ju-late-ing. Then I realized I sounded like an idiot. Could I have thought of anything more stupid to say? Maybe. The guy was gorgeous, and my IQ was dropping into my panties.

I was at the Sportsman's Expo, alone. I'd seen the ads on TV and in the newspaper, and guessed it would be prime hunting ground for men. Neither Louise nor Cassie had wanted to come with me, and I'd thought myself too shy to go alone, and had put it out of my mind, deciding there'd only be rednecks there anyway.

But then, driving back into town after an appointment, I'd passed the Expo Center and seen the parking lot full of cars, and the same insanity that had struck me in front of The Purple Palace struck me again, and not believing I was doing it, I turned off into the lot.

I could only hope this adventure would be less embarrassing than The Purple Palace had been. Thank the merciful gods, the interview with me in the parking lot had not been part of the story that aired.

I hadn't used the vibrator yet. Just thinking about the thing brought on flashbacks, not to mention concerns about the bacteria on that clerk's hands.

Now here I was, a single female in a sea of aluminum fishing boats and forests of hunting gear. There was a trout pond for kids to fish, demonstrations of hunting dogs retrieving decoys, tent cities and enough outdoor gadgetry to make Scott a happy camper.

And now there was this guy who looked younger than me, leaning one hand against the base of the raised salmon tank and standing close enough I could smell his aftershave.

Ohhhhh, baby.

I remembered my discussion with Scott about instant attraction. I had never felt it as strongly as I was right now. What would it be like to touch those shoulders?

"I don't fish, myself. I came with some buddies of mine. They've got some good hiking gear here, though. Have you seen it?"

Obviously an invitation. "No, not yet."

He took my arm, and I barely restrained myself from leaning against him as he pulled me toward the gear. He was so good-looking, it seemed that even having him touch my arm should send me into convulsions of sexual pleasure. It didn't, but just breathing in the scent of him was better than a vibrator.

He had dark ash hair and blue eyes, a square jaw that was a little too wide and a nose a little too flat, but my God, his body. I let him drag me over to the backpacks and boots, wool socks and hiking poles.

"Do you hike much?" he asked.

"Just day hikes, Forest Park, the gorge, sometimes Silver Falls."

"Those trails in Forest Park, you can't really call those hiking," he said. "You have to go out into the national forests, and I don't just mean around Mt. Hood, although there are plenty of beautiful trails there. Have you heard of the Pacific Crest Trail? I did about three hundred miles of it a couple years back, before I joined the Bureau."

"The Bureau?" I emerged long enough from my stew of hormones to inquire into his profession. A girl had to have standards, however beautiful the body.

"I'm with the Portland Police Bureau. Does that bother you?"

Ohhhh…uniforms. "No, it doesn't bother me at all." Big man with gun. Protector of the innocent. Catch bad guys, run down muggers and rapists, save damsels in distress.

A whole future flitted before my eyes. We'd live in a suburban home, holding summer barbecues in the backyard where a dozen hunky cops would hang out drinking beer from the bottles, their wives in white cotton tops and brightly colored capri pants, grouped together talking about the kids.

We'd have two kids of our own, and he'd be one of those dads who is great playing with them, and looks adorable feeding one a bottle, but is too much of a guy to turn into one of those feminine fathers who gets pasty and pudgy and walks around with a towel to catch spit-up thrown over his shoulder.

Then the novelty of the baby would wear off, and he'd be too caught up in work to spend time with them until the boy hit the teens. Then there'd be shouting matches, fiery hot testosterone floating through the air, our daughter and I keeping our heads low. Family vacations would be filled with tension, more work than pleasure, creating the memories that would keep a kid from coming home for Thanksgiving once he or she was grown.

Then he'd get shot on duty, and I'd be a grieving widow living off his pension.

"Good. Some people get weird about it, you know what I mean?" he said. "They think I'm going to arrest them for something."

"Even women?"

He grinned, showing white, wide teeth that belonged on a model. "Nah, guys mostly. Every guy has *something* he doesn't want the cops to find out about."

"Like what?" I asked, taking the bait.

"Unpaid traffic tickets, pot in his sock drawer, a gun under the front seat of his car. Maybe he picked up a hooker once, or downloaded something he's not sure is legal from the Internet."

"All guys can't have secrets like that," I said, thinking of all the men I had exchanged e-mail with, and considered dating. Maybe they were all freaks, and two or three were stalking me, and I was too innocent to know it until some night they sprung out of the bushes and attacked. "Picking up prostitutes? No one our age does that, do they?"

"You'd be surprised by the scum out there. I'll bet there are at least a dozen guys in here with outstanding warrants, and another dozen who are out on parole."

I inched closer to him. "Really?"

"When you're a cop, you have to stay alert all the time. Some of these guys, you bust them, then you testify against them in court, and when they're convicted they swear they're going to come get you when they get out. I never know when I'm going to come across someone I put in jail."

"What would you do?" I asked, looking around me at the men who had started to take on a sinister air.

"I'm always ready."

"What, do you carry a gun?"

"Always."

"You're kidding," I said, leaning away from him now.

"No way am I kidding."

"Where is it?" I asked, looking him over.

"Ankle holster. I have a knife, too."

"Why?"

"You see the things I have, you want to be safe. Something happens with the gun, I want a backup." He looked at me, and seemed to catch that he was not being reassuring. "Hey, I'm one of the good guys. You never have to worry about *me*."

"No?"

"Hell no. Mr. Clean, that's who I am. You gotta have self-respect. You see the dirt bags out there, and you don't want to do anything to put you in the same category.''

"You never even speed?"

"I don't get caught," he said, flashing me another cover-boy grin.

"And you never download porn from the Internet?"

"You show me a guy with access to a computer, and I'll bet you a hundred bucks he's downloaded porn at least once. Some things you gotta accept as normal. But only a loser is going to spend his nights alone in front of the screen, getting off."

"Not you, huh?"

"I prefer real life," he said, looking me in the eye.

The conversation had degenerated to sexual innuendo, and it was my own fault. I knew better: you mention anything sexual, then a guy knows you're thinking about sex, and he assumes he's got a chance of getting it.

Which this guy might. He seemed to have pheromones oozing out his pores.

"I'm Pete," he said, stopping and holding out his hand.

I shook it. "Hannah."

"Do you have a pair of good hiking boots, Hannah?" he asked as we stopped in front of a display.

"No. I usually hike in old tennis shoes."

"Let's find a pair. I've gotta take you hiking, on a real trail."

I let him lead me to his favorite brand, and hold up options. Who was I to protest? But then I did want to protest, when I saw the price tag.

"A hundred and seventy-five dollars? I don't know, that's a little too much. I'm self-employed."

"Are you? Well, how about this pair," he said, holding up a pair of royal-blue mesh-and-suede boots. "They're lightweight. Not one hundred percent waterproof, but they should dry quickly."

It seemed a little odd he hadn't asked me what I did for a living. Most people, you say you're self-employed, and they want to know what you do. But he was a guy, after all, and he was at least paying me attention by trying to find me a good pair of shoes.

The blue boots were only eighty dollars, which seemed a bargain considering the prices on the others, so I gave in and bought them. That new hemming machine would have to wait a little longer.

"You want to go get a bite to eat?" Pete asked. "I'm starved."

"Sure." The guy moved at lightning speed. A meal, vague plans to go hiking…was he always like this, or had I swept him off his feet?

Ha, ha. Yeah, right.

"You don't mind driving, do you? I came with my buds, and my car's at home."

"No, that's fine," I said, and a second later regretted it, realizing I'd just agreed to let a strange guy toting both a gun and a knife into my car. He must have seen the look on my face.

"Hey, if it'll make you feel better…" he said, then dug his wallet out of his pocket and showed me his badge. "I'm not a freak."

It could be fake, but I believed him anyway. I was even more reassured when he dragged me over to his friends, who looked like clean-cut guys. They looked like the type I would have hated in high school, wearing baseball caps with the brims bent into a perfect arch, wraparound mirrored sunglasses resting against the crowns. They were smirky, cool guys, brains for nothing but sports, but they probably weren't psychotic criminals.

Probably.

"This is Hannah, we're going to get out of here and go grab something to eat."

"Nice to meet you, Hannah," one of them said, and shook my hand in a surprising display of manners and apparent warmth.

The others grinned, their posing postures showing they thought they were pretty adult at their vast age of twenty-two or twenty-three, or however old they were. "Don't let Pete sweet-talk you," one of the snotty-looking ones said. "He's one smooth dude when he wants to be."

"Dude"?

I grinned sickly back, knowing they were thinking I was about to be Pete's latest conquest. My enthusiasm for the impromptu lunch faded.

"Hey, don't let them get to you," Pete said, leading me toward the doors, and showing a perception I'd assumed he lacked. "They're good guys, but they need to grow up."

"You know that I'm older than you, don't you?" I asked, feeling insecure and uncertain about all of this.

"I guessed. What are you, twenty-seven, twenty-eight?"

"Almost thirty. How old are you?"

"Twenty-five."

Only a year older than Cassie's fresh catch. Now I

couldn't hassle her anymore. I knew I should listen to my own advice and drop the acquaintance right now, only he was *sooo* cute. And seemed so interested.

"What is it with younger guys, going out with older women?" I asked as we wound our way through the parking lot toward my car.

"You really want to know?"

"Yeah."

"You've got your shit together. Girls my age, they're so needy, they cling to you like an octopus, you can never get them off. Older women, you're more independent."

I wondered if that meant he thought we needed less attention. "I'd think you'd want those younger bodies," I said. "No cellulite, no droop."

"The bodies are good, but they don't know what to do with them. Older chicks, they know how to work it."

"I always thought it would be fun to play Mrs. Robinson, just once," I said, somewhat lacking in enthusiasm.

"Who?"

"Never mind."

We found my car and got in, and he fiddled with the radio, switching stations and messing with the speaker settings as I drove out of the lot. "Where are we going?" I asked.

"How about pizza? There's a place on Broadway I like."

"Sure." Pizza didn't seem like date food—nothing you ate with your hands and risked getting stuck in your teeth was date food, not to mention the garlic—but I suppose pizza is what one should expect from a twenty-five-year-old.

We talked about music and movies on the drive, and books once we were at the restaurant and waiting for our food.

"I love to read," Pete said.

"Real books? Not just magazines?"

"Oh, yeah. I'm reading *The Grapes of Wrath* right now."

I was impressed. Maybe there was more to him than the body and the aftershave. Not that there had to be— I was still enjoying letting my eyes slip from his face to his shoulders, the same way a guy had a hard time keeping his gaze off a woman's breasts. He was wearing a blue chambray button-down shirt over a white T-shirt, and the cotton looked more than warm and soft enough to touch. My hands would just barely span the thickness of those shoulders.

Ohhh...

"Are you from around here?" he asked, breaking into my lustful musings.

"Roseburg. I've lived in Oregon all my life."

"I'm from Ohio. I like it out here, especially the mountains. But I'm thinking of moving up to Seattle, or maybe down to San Francisco."

"You are? Why?" I asked, faintly alarmed. I didn't want to think of this lovely piece of manhood leaving anytime soon.

"There's just not enough happening here. In my work, I mean. Not enough excitement. That's why I became a cop to begin with. I've got ADHD, Attention

Deficit Hyperactivity Disorder, and I thought it would provide the right type of stimulation.''

I blinked at him. He was attention-deficit and hyperactive. I hadn't known anyone with that particular problem, and didn't know what it might mean to any future relationship.

''Don't worry, I take medication for it, it's under control. It just leaves me with a lot of energy. I have to be doing things.''

''Oh. Okay.''

The pizza came and we ate about half of it, me drinking root beer and Pete the real stuff. I wondered what effect that would have on his medication. I went to the bathroom, and when I returned to the table the leftovers had been wrapped in foil and the bill paid.

''Can you leave the tip? I used the last of my cash.''

''Sure.'' I put a couple dollars on the table, wondering why he hadn't put the whole thing on a credit or debit card. Maybe he liked paying cash. Whatever.

Between his age, the ADHD and his comments about moving to another city, I knew he'd about reached his quota of red flags, but none of those things seemed big enough to warrant giving up on him just yet.

Or maybe I was just unwilling to give up those shoulders. Women weren't supposed to be so affected by a beautiful body—we were supposed to have our eyes on a guy's earning potential—but damn, he was one gorgeous piece of flesh. Since I'd never had my hands on such a specimen before, I thought I could be excused the lapse in practicality.

''You want to pick up a movie or something?'' he asked as we headed back to the car.

"I'm not sure..." I said, thinking of the pile of alterations waiting for me at home. Butler & Sons had had a sale on men's pants, and I had about forty pairs waiting to be hemmed.

"Aw, sure you do," he said, putting an arm around my shoulders. "I've got to work tomorrow, this will be my only chance to see you for almost a week."

He sounded so eager—so enamored—I couldn't say no. We headed off to the video store, rented *Meet the Parents,* then he directed me back to his apartment, which was in a newish complex in Southeast Portland.

Kids yelled and ran in the winding drive and parking areas between wood-sided buildings, balls and bikes appearing in front of my car like scenes from a driving test.

"Lots of families live here?" I asked.

"Huh? Yeah. Well, lots of single mothers. It all looks okay, but I tell you, some funny stuff goes on. Doesn't matter how clean a place looks, there's dirt if you know where to find it."

The kids looked pretty innocent to me. "Like what?"

"Drug dealing. Domestic violence. God, I hate those dirt bags who beat their wives. I tell you, when I see that, I get *this* close—" here he held up his thumb and index finger, a centimeter apart "—*this* close to pounding the guy into the ground. Of all the low things to do, beating a woman. Or a kid. They should give us a license to shoot the scum, and do society a favor."

I parked where he pointed, and we climbed the outside stairs to his door on the third floor.

It was good to despise wife beaters and child abusers, and I supposed I should have had my heart thumping at his display of manly protective instincts, but somehow his vehemence had left me less admiring rather than more. Maybe his opinions seemed too simple, his targets too easy, and perhaps too calculated to win female approval.

Or maybe he really did feel that strongly. And maybe it was all that pent-up energy that came off him, that made me uncomfortable.

"Fluffy-Ass!" he cried, opening the door.

I gaped. Whose ass was fluffy? Not mine, thank you very much!

He bent, then turned around with a giant gray flop-eared rabbit in his arms. Any faint alarms about his vehemence or the gun on his ankle were washed clean away. The guy had a bunny.

Who couldn't adore a gorgeous guy with a bunny?

"This is Frank, the Fluffy-Ass Rabbit," Pete said, and handed him to me.

I sagged under the weight of Frank, who was at least ten pounds heavier than any rabbit had a right to be. His rear claws dug into my belly, his front claws scraping at my forearm until we found a mutually satisfying position. I followed Pete into his apartment, thinking that bunnies were far more cuddly to look at than to hold.

"How long have you had him?" I asked.

"Watch your step!"

I side-stepped, looking down and seeing a scattering of round rabbit droppings.

"Frank, you bad-ass rabbit," Pete said, going into the kitchen and returning with a paper towel, with which he picked up the pellets. "He's house-trained, but I swear he does this to spite me. He belonged to my ex, but she moved in with a friend with a Rottweiler. Frank would have been Dog Chow in a week.''

''Does your ex, ah...have visitation?''

He looked up from where he was kneeling, towel full of bunny poop. ''Janet? Yeah, she comes by sometimes, but I try not to be here when she does. She still has a thing for me.''

''Oh.'' She must be one of those sticky octopus girls he was talking about. I wondered if he was telling me as a warning not to be the same, or if he was bragging that no woman could live without him.

''She's got to just let it go, you know? It's not good for her. She leaves me notes on my windshield, drops off gifts at the Bureau. It's embarrassing.''

''The other guys give you a hard time?''

''They have no respect for privacy. Some chick leaves flowers for you, you can bet they'll read the card and give you shit for a week.''

''They sound charming.''

''They're good guys, it's just their way to blow off steam.''

He went to go throw the paper towel away. When Frank struggled I set him down, then brushed at the bits of hair clinging to my clothes, and rubbed at the scratches on my arms.

''Want anything to drink?'' Pete asked from the kitchen.

''Ice water would be nice,'' I said, and took the opportunity to look around.

The room was cleaner than I'd expected, the carpet fairly new and beige, the walls white, miniblinds on the windows. He had some sort of multipurpose weight-lifting machine taking up a third of the space, but the rest looked reasonable for a guy his age. Futon couch—of course—television, a mediocre sound system and, surprisingly, a large bookcase with books in it.

I'd thought he'd been exaggerating about the reading. I went closer to browse the titles, and as I did, realized there was something funny about the spines of the books. They weren't spines at all.

They were boxes.

I pulled one out. It was a book on tape. I looked at all the rest. There were a few real books on the shelves, but most were tapes.

"Hey, Pete," I said as he came out of the kitchen and handed me the glass of ice water. "I thought you said you liked to read. These are all tapes."

"Same thing, isn't it? It's all the same words."

I frowned. It didn't seem the same to me, somehow, although I couldn't say precisely why not.

"It's the ADHD," he said. "It's hard to sit still and read a book in print, but I can listen to a tape while I'm working out or driving."

"Oh." It still seemed like cheating to me. It was great he listened to books, he probably knew more of the classics than I did, from the look of his shelves, yet somehow I felt he was cheating, saying he loved to read. Seemed he should be claiming a great love of being told stories, instead.

Well, at least he liked stories, and not just tech magazines or sports television.

We put the tape in, turned down the lights and settled

down to watch the movie. Frank hopped his way out of the room, disappearing through a half-open door.

Five minutes into the movie Pete leaned against me. Ten minutes, and his arm was around me. At fifteen minutes he turned toward me.

"Can I kiss you?"

I thought about it for a moment. What was a kiss? It couldn't hurt. "Okay."

He went to work on my mouth, and with my mind half on *Meet the Parents* and half on his body, I let my hands roam over his shoulders and his back.

Pete sucked at my neck and licked my ear. I listened to the movie, and wondered why this wasn't more exciting. With that gorgeous body, touching and being touched should have had me moaning on the floor.

Shouldn't it?

He squeezed my breasts, then sent a hand roaming up my shirt. He pulled a cup of my bra down, and pulled at my nipple. To no effect.

He rolled us over so that he was lying beneath me, me straddling his hips, and started using both hands on my breasts. I let him continue, wondering when I was going to start getting excited.

In the background Ben Stiller started talking about his life on the farm, and I smiled.

"What?"

"Nothing."

He pushed up my shirt and, leaning forward, took the tip of a breast in his mouth, lightly chomping on it. I looked down at his head and spotted a couple premature gray hairs. Ben Stiller was describing milking a cat. I loved this part.

He leaned back again and, putting his hands on my hips, started to grind me against him. "I want to be inside you," he said.

I grinned, listening to the dialogue.

"Want to move into the bedroom?"

My attention swung back to where it should have been. "I hardly know you," I said.

"God, you feel so good."

I shifted, rubbing my crotch against him. He closed his eyes and made a fake-sounding moan. I hadn't done it to please him; I was trying to tell if he had an erection. I couldn't feel anything I could be sure of, except his jeans zipper.

Was there a reason I was getting gyped out of erections on dates? Was this another example of synchronicity? And I hadn't been able to use the vibrator, either. Maybe that meant something.

"I think we should get to know each other better first, don't you?" I said as I debated taking him up on his bedroom offer, anyway. I'd never had a one-night stand before, and wondered if it would be worth trying, given the proper latex and chemical precautions.

Then again, given my present lack of arousal, it seemed doomed to be disappointing.

"Yeah, you're right," he said, stopping his hip-grinding and opening his eyes. "You're just so damn hot," he said, looking hopeful.

I dismounted, and snuggled down beside him, full-length, on the futon. I could let my hand play over his chest this way, which was all I really wanted to do at this point, anyway.

He put his arm around me. "I'm working the late

shift, four to midnight, this week, but my next day off, you want to go do something? We can go to the beach maybe, or for a hike.''

"That'd be great.''

"You can get the time off?''

"I'm self-employed, remember?''

He grunted.

The movie played on in the background, and I let my hand explore his slack muscles. His breathing started to change, his body going even more limp. I raised up on one elbow.

He was asleep.

I made a face, and rolled off the couch. He woke up.

"Are you leaving?''

"I've got to get going.''

He dragged himself upright. "You've got to leave me your phone number.''

I dug out a business card and handed it to him. He took it, stood up and shoved it in a pocket, then walked me out to my car and gave me a hug.

"I'll call you,'' he said, "we'll go out and do something.''

I nodded as if I believed him, and left.

Seventeen

Pink Panties

"I can never decide," I said.

"Neither can I," Louise said, hunkered down beside me in front of the dessert cabinet at Papa Haydn's, the restaurant in NW Portland that was the mothership for dessert lovers.

Cakes and tortes and layered meringues seven-, eight-, nine-inches high sat behind glass, their names either written in chocolate on the edge of the plate or in gold pen on cards tucked into an edge. There were low, dense, chocolatey things, fruit tarts, gelato, even a baked Alaska.

"I have to go look at the menu again," I said, and we went back to our table to read the details of what we'd been looking at.

It was Friday afternoon, and Louise had called in sick to work this morning, taking a mental health day. Her employer was the only one I knew of that actually let people do that, but I suppose, being a crisis center, they needed their employees to be fully functioning.

And Louise was not functioning. There was a shopping bag of excruciatingly expensive lingerie sitting beneath our table, waiting to be returned to a boutique down the street. It had turned out that she was not going to have a reason to wear it.

We placed our orders, and settled down to that business of women: talk.

"Last night we went out to dinner again," Louise said. She had shadows under her eyes. They did not go well with freckles.

"What was this, the third time?"

Her eyes shifted away, and she fiddled with the pot of tea the waitress had brought her. "Fourth time, and we went to see a movie Monday." She looked at me. "I was afraid to tell you. I thought you'd scold me."

"Who am I to scold? As if I've done anything wise recently."

"Pete still hasn't called?"

"No. Not that I expected him to."

"But still. I mean, he seemed like he liked you, didn't he?"

"I thought so. Apparently only enough to try to sleep with me, though," I said.

"Men. I just don't understand them."

"You have a master's in psychology."

"Lot of good it's done me."

"So what happened? You went out to dinner last night with Derek and...?"

"And I was getting impatient. I've been thinking about him all the time, I can't concentrate on my work, I'm daydreaming about our future together, about kissing him, wondering what it would be like to have sex with him... But I didn't know what he was thinking, what he was feeling, if anything. I mean, he'd been going out with me, yeah, but he hadn't made any definite moves. He'd say things that I thought meant he was interested, but then nothing would happen.''

''Mixed signals.''

''Exactly.''

The waitress appeared with our desserts: Louise had some sort of eight-layer chocolate cake with a gold-flecked coffee bean stuck atop a swirl of dense chocolate frosting, and I had *panna cotta,* an Italian custard with raspberries and sauce.

''So I decided to try to be subtle,'' Louise said, after she'd taken a couple bites and we'd exchanged samples. ''We were sitting at the restaurant, waiting for our food, and I told him about these dreams I'd had.''

''Uh-oh. Real dreams?''

''Yeah, uh-oh, real dreams. The first wasn't so bad. I got a flat tire, called him, and he came and changed the tire for me.''

''Your own personal Triple-A.''

''I have Triple-A, too. You'd think if I pay for it, why not use it? But anyway, that dream was all right to talk about. After all, we're counselors, we like to analyze dreams. He thought it meant I felt I could rely on him, and seemed flattered.''

''Dream number two?''

''Dream number two, and three. This is where the trouble begins. In Dream Two we're standing in line somewhere, and I wrap my arms around his waist and lay my head on his chest.''

''Oh, dear. How did he react?''

''He got a strange little half smile on his lips. I took it as encouragement.''

I grimaced, dreading what was coming.

"Yeah. Dream Three, we were in the shower together, having sex."

"You told him that?" I asked, aghast.

"Yes. And idiot that I am, then I asked him, 'How do you feel about that?'"

I forgot about my *panna cotta*. "Oh, Louise, no."

"Yes." She mashed frosting with her fork. "Everything got *real* quiet, like we were in this little pocket of silence in the middle of the restaurant, and I could feel my face getting hot, my neck, my chest. I wanted to just slide under the table, find a nice dark place and hide."

"What'd he say?"

She met my eyes, leaving off the cake killing. "He said—are you ready?—'Did I miss something? Some sort of cue?'"

"Oh, Louise..."

"Then he says, 'I'm sorry, I've really got to go to the bathroom.' And he gets up and leaves me at the table."

"Ah...Christ. How embarrassing."

"Try humiliating. So there I sat, twiddling my toes, and the food comes and he's still not back, and there's no way I feel like eating now."

"But he did come back?"

"Yes. I don't know what he was doing in there all that time. Throwing up, maybe. Laughing his ass off. Thinking about bolting. I don't know. But he dealt with it as best as I think any guy could be expected to. He sat back down and took my hand, and said, 'We're going to talk this out.'"

"I think I'd have preferred to drop it and go home," I said. "Pretend like it never happened."

She shrugged. "I give him credit for sticking around."

"So what did you two decide in the end?"

"There's been no real decision. At least, not on his part."

"What?"

"He started asking me questions about what I wanted in life, if I wanted children—which of course I don't— asked if I wanted to get married someday, asked what I was looking for in a man."

"Almost like he was seeing if he could fit the job," I said.

"At the end of it all, he said he was 'confused,' and he had to think about all this."

"'Confused,' huh?"

"Confused. Anytime a guy says he's confused, I take it to mean he doesn't want to be with you. Maybe he likes you as a casual friend, maybe he likes pouring his heart out to you because you're stupid enough to sit there and listen and sympathize, but he doesn't want you."

"Why can't they just come out and say that?" I asked.

"If they did, they'd lose their backup girl, the one they know they could have if they asked. I'm not going to sit around for that. I've got *some* self-respect, after all."

"You think that's really what it is, he just wants to keep you in his back pocket?" I asked.

"Guys do it all the time. Hell, I've done it to guys myself."

"Why'd he ask you all that stuff about what you wanted?"

"He's jerking me around. He doesn't mean to, but it's what he's doing. He's never going to really want me," she said, and her voice caught.

"You sound so sure," I said quietly. It was never good to see a friend hurt.

"I am sure. If I wait around for him to become un-confused, all I'll be doing is torturing myself. The only way I can regain some control, some *power,* dammit, is to make the decision myself. My head knows it's the right thing to do. I just wish my heart followed." She mashed cake with her fork, and her lower lip trembled. "I wish I could stop hoping for a better ending."

The lingerie boutique was in an old house on NW 23rd, one of the trendy streets lined with shops for over-priced housewares, nightclub clothing, handmade dog biscuits, scented candles, and the odd shop of imports from Indonesia, India, China, or Africa. Mid-size decid-uous trees lined the street, strung year-round with white Christmas lights, and between the browsing possibilities and the coffee shops on every block, it was a popular place to meet, people-watch, or just waste time.

We weren't far from where Scott lived, and I was planning to stop by his place later to pick up some pants he needed altered. There were new streetcars running from downtown to this neighborhood, up and running for only half a year, and if Scott had wished, he could have taken one of them to work instead of his bicycle. But I'd seen his legs, and could see why the bike held his favor.

We climbed the wooden stairs to Belinda's Fine European Lingerie, and opened the door to silken, perfumed luxury.

"Can you believe I paid twenty-eight dollars for a pair of underpants?" Louise asked as we went to the counter. "What was I thinking?"

"Can I see them?"

She pulled them out of the bag, the price tag dangling from the hip. They were pale pink silk, with cream lace insets, and they were beautiful.

"And the bra—we don't need to say how much the bra was."

I knew there was also a teddy and a nightgown in the bag, still wrapped in tissue. I hadn't asked to see them only because I thought it would be too upsetting for Louise. The high-priced underwear—at least we could talk about the cost of such a tiny scrap of silk, without dwelling on the shattered hopes.

She handed the bag to the clerk behind the counter, along with the receipt. "I can't believe I was so *stupid*. God." Then she started talking to the clerk, explaining about the return. I drifted away to browse through the merchandise.

I didn't often find my way to the small boutiques outside of the heart of downtown, and I saw what I'd been missing. The prices were, as always, beyond my pocketbook, but a girl could dream, even if she couldn't see herself trying to sew her own bra or merry widow. Not that I couldn't do it; I just couldn't bother.

The negligees were achingly lovely, and unlike the foundation garments they were possible to reproduce, if one could find the same quality of lace. I went through a rack of gowns with an assessing eye, examining seams and cut.

My dream wedding dress was still in the paper pattern stages. It occurred to me that with a wedding dress one also needed something for the wedding night, a bit of sensuous luxury in flowing pastel.

If you sew it, he will come.

The words whispering in my head seemed more appropriate than ever.

Louise found me. "They made me take store credit," she said, her mouth in an unhappy twist. "I don't even want to think about wearing underwear, not from here. Why bother wearing any at all, for that matter? Who's ever going to see it?"

"You have a problem with underwear?" I asked.

"Half the time you don't really need it. It's all a scam."

"I'm not wearing any," I said. "A bra, but no panties."

"You're kidding."

"Am I?" I hadn't had any that were clean this morning, so I'd worn a long tailored skirt. Who was going to know the difference? "You know, there's a place for people like you, Louise. Underwear Anonymous. I'm surprised you haven't heard of it."

She started to smile. "First I'd have to admit I had a problem."

"Do you need to wear underwear to relax in a social situation? Do you put it on before going out? Do you wear it every day?"

"Yes!" Louise said.

"Has underwear caused you emotional trauma?"

"It's doing so at this very moment," she said.

"Then you need Underwear Anonymous."

She giggled, looking a little more like the Louise I knew. There wasn't much that could keep her down for long. She was so much her own person, so content in her own private space, I sometimes wondered if she would ever marry. It was hard to imagine her sharing her space with anyone. I almost wondered if she'd chosen Derek because she knew, deep down, that nothing was going to come of it.

Louise looked around the store, then back at me. "You know, it's too bad they don't make this type of stuff for men. The fanciest they get is silk boxers, and how does that compare in price? Just another bit of male/female inequality showing itself."

"What do you want? Guys in codpieces?"

"Wouldn't that be something?" she asked as we left the shop and started down the sidewalk. "Wouldn't you love to see guys walking around with those stuck to the front of their pants? I'll bet they'd wear them, too."

"Nah, what we need is a modern version," I said. "Something that doesn't look like it came off a portrait of Henry VIII. We need some sort of…weenie wrap."

"What, like a scarf?"

"More like a sock," I said, envisioning it. "In bright colors, made of spandex. Or polar fleece, for winter. They could wear them attached to those tight pants runners wear."

"I don't think they'd like that. Too much flopping around."

"Well, okay, then it could just be underwear like a teddy, worn only to impress one's date. It could have a little pouch for the balls, and all tie on with a ribbon. Not many women think a penis is pretty, anyway. Why not spruce it up a bit?''

"I think I'd prefer the bare thing," Louise said.

"No, this could be great. I could get a stall at Saturday Market and sell them."

"They'd throw you out."

"I could advertise in the back of *Cosmo*."

"That might work," she admitted. "Be sure to offer them in different sizes, and put a big XXXL tag on the big ones everyone will buy."

"And an XXS on the ones sold as revenge gifts to ex-lovers," I said. And in my mind I was thinking that Louise needed a Voodoo Derek doll.

"Hannah, you are a warped individual, you do know that, don't you?"

"You wouldn't have me any other way."

Eighteen

Tapestry with Fringe

"Aren't you going to measure my inseam?" Scott asked as I knelt at his feet and pinned the cuffs of his pants.

"No, I don't need to."

"Damn. I was looking forward to that all day."

I raised a brow at him. "Shouldn't your lawyer lady be taking care of all those sorts of needs?"

"There's no fun in thinking about that. But a seamstress, with a tape measure, reaching up your leg, now that's something to fantasize about."

"I'd think that would frighten the average man, having a ruler so close."

"Not me."

I snorted. "No one would ever suspect that dentists were such horn dogs."

"We're good with our hands," he said, leering.

"Next," I said, and he stepped behind his kitchen counter to take off the pants and put on a new pair. "I've got a joke for you."

He groaned.

"This dentist is looking at the films from his female

patient's mouth, and he says, 'Uh-oh, cavities. We're going to have to do a lot of drilling.' The woman sort of moans, and says, 'Oh, God, I'd rather give birth to a child.' So the dentist says, 'In that case, let me adjust the chair.'" I grinned at him.

"Where do you *get* these lame jokes?"

"Off the Internet. Where else?"

He came back over to me in the new pants.

"You know, Scott, you could have had the store hem these for you. I'm sure it was included in the price."

"I trust you to do it. I wanted to talk to you about making some pillows for my couch, too. My living room looks too...I don't know. Cold."

I looked over my shoulder at the area in question. "You've got a black leather couch and a glass coffee table. Of course it looks cold."

"You'll help me, won't you? And maybe one of those cover things for my comforter."

"A duvet, you mean?"

"I guess. Maybe you could help me choose paint, too? You're good with color."

I finished pinning and stood. "I'd be glad to help, but I don't know that you'd like what I chose. I look at a room, and I'm more likely to think of how I would want to live, rather than how someone else would."

"That's okay."

He went back to the kitchen to put on his old pants, and I sat on the couch, kicking my shoes off and putting my legs up, to enjoy the leather and the view from his windows, which looked out over the northern end of the city, with a glimpse of the Willamette River. I could get used to a view like that.

Louise and I had browsed the shops on 23rd for a while, then she'd gone home on the streetcar, and I'd driven to a specialty trim and fabric store that I'd heard about but never visited, and killed an hour there until it was time to come to Scott's.

I looked around, checking for signs of the lawyer. There were none apparent, no stockings trailing out from under the couch cushions, no mushy card on the mantel above the gas fireplace, no forgotten pair of feminine sunglasses on the counter. The real place to check would be the master bath, but I didn't have any reason to go in there.

Not that it mattered if she'd left signs behind. What did I care?

"So how *is* it going with Ms. Law?"

"All right," Scott said, coming over to join me. I pulled my feet up, but he stopped me. "It's okay," he said, and sat and pulled my feet into his lap. He tickled the sole.

"Knock it off!" I said, punching his thigh with my free heel. He started massaging my toes, and it felt too good to protest. "So, things with her are moving along?" I asked, resuming the topic. I wasn't going to let him escape it.

"She doesn't have a lot of free time, so we go out maybe once a week. Her job's pretty demanding. She has a lot of funny stories to tell, though. A lot funnier than I have, looking in mouths all day."

"She's outgoing?"

"She's entertaining, and opinionated. You know she's not going to take any garbage from anyone."

I wondered if I took garbage, and if so, just how unattractive it was. My overused dentist jokes could hardly compare to courtroom dramas for entertainment value, either.

"Do you think there might be a future with her?"

"I don't know."

"Still?"

"Still," he said.

"Is she pretty?"

"She looks like Lucy Lawless."

"You're kidding."

"I'm not."

"Huh," I said, and felt the need to compete. "I had a date with a cop."

His hands on my toes stopped. "When?"

I told him the story, skimming over the part when Pete had his hands on my breasts and where I'd tried to feel if he had an erection hidden in his jeans somewhere, but letting Scott get the gist of what had occurred.

"No harm done," I said in conclusion. "A little kissing and groping, he falls asleep, never calls. Oh, well. Move on."

"You know, you can get herpes from kissing."

"Thanks for reminding me," I said, not meaning it.

"Did he have any sores around his mouth?"

"You think I would have kissed him, if he did? So at least I should be safe. It's not contagious when the sores aren't there, right?"

"They could have been inside his mouth. Or maybe he was at the beginning of an outbreak, and they weren't visible yet."

"Are you trying to freak me out?" I asked.

"Tuberculosis. Hand, foot and mouth disease."

"What the hell is that? Isn't that something sheep get?"

"That's foot and mouth, or hoof and mouth. Hand, foot and mouth gives you blisters on those parts. It's a virus."

"I've never heard of it."

"Mostly kids get it," he said.

"I'm not going to be French kissing any kids."

"Then there's syphilis."

"People still get that? Didn't it go the way of small-pox?" I asked.

"Not hardly."

"You're going to put me off kissing entirely. I'm going to be reduced to hugs and holding hands." I was beginning to get a slimy feeling, as though maybe I should have rinsed with a shot of whiskey when I'd gotten home. Not that we had whiskey in our house. Cranberry juice?

"Hugs are probably safer, but I don't want you picking up scabies."

"For God's sake. The more you talk, the less I believe anything you say." I lightly kicked him on the thigh, then sat up. "I should probably get going."

"You don't have to. I have stuff for dinner." I looked at him, and he quickly went on, "I'll feed you as thanks for coming over and doing my pants. It's bribery, is all, since I want you to fit my pillows and duvet into your schedule, too."

"Do you have any idea of a color scheme? Or a style?" I asked, although what I really wanted to know was what was going on here. We had known each other for so long, I could not tell if he was coming on to me or just being friendly. Maybe he didn't want to spend the evening alone, and wanted company the same as I might enjoy having Louise over for dinner, or might like drinking tea and chatting with Cassie.

And maybe he was flirting a little bit, the same way I flirted a little bit with him, because we both knew nothing would ever come of it. It was safe. He was Louise's ex, and would always, in some way, belong to her.

I couldn't come right out and ask him if his interest went beyond the platonic, as whatever the answer was, the question itself would put a bruise on the friendship, creating a tender spot we would have to avoid. So, I might as well try to not think about it.

Easier said than done, of course.

"I don't know, something warm," Scott was saying. "I don't like these ones I have, they're ugly," he said, slapping one of the light green linen-covered pillows on the couch. "I don't know why I bought them."

"I don't, either," I said. He had them in green and in white, with dull metal buttons fastening the open end. "I could use the pillow forms you have, and just recover them. It'll be cheaper. Price limit?"

"How much can pillow covers cost?"

"Louise and I saw some pillows in one of the shops on 23rd today that were over two hundred dollars."

He gaped at me. "Each?"

"Aaa, don't worry. It won't cost you quite that much," I said, grinning. "Maybe you'll have to pull a few extra teeth to pay me, though."

"I could always trade you dental services. We could barter the price."

"I don't think so," I said, my stomach doing a sickening flip at the mere thought.

He gave me one of those looks parents use on children who have given a particularly lame excuse for why they don't need to eat their Brussels sprouts, and then got up to make dinner.

I offered to help, but he shooed me away, and instead I examined his living room and thought about what types of fabrics I might want to use on the pillows. Tapestry would be nice, and a rich gold fringe.

"Mind if I go in your bedroom?" I asked. "To get ideas for the duvet."

He stopped where he was, a bowl of something from the refrigerator in his hands.

"I won't pry," I said. "And I promise not to notice any dirty underwear."

"Just...just let me do a quick cleanup," he said, putting the bowl on the counter and dashing ahead of me into his room. I listened to him rooting about, closet doors opening and closing, footsteps thudding across the hardwood floor. I frowned, wondering why, if he'd known ahead of time that he wanted me to make a duvet, he hadn't picked up his room so I could look at it.

Finally he emerged. "Okay," he said, looking frightened.

"Got the porn stashed?"

His eyes widened.

"That cop said all guys look at porn."

"Not *all* guys."

"That's not a denial."

"I refuse to testify against myself," he said.

"Oh, for heaven's sake. Go make me dinner," I said,

and slipped past him into his room. He stared after me, and I shooed him with my hands until he left.

And I was alone in the sacred male bower.

I felt the temptation to pry, to dig through drawers and medicine cabinets, to look under the bed, but it was a small temptation and easily resisted. I couldn't betray his trust like that, without feeling dirty.

Although I *would* like to know if there was a sealed box of condoms somewhere, inching toward its expiration date, a latex and cardboard symbol of hope and disappointment. I didn't want to imagine Scott having sex with someone, but I did want to think he at least wanted to do it. For some reason, I liked the image of him pining away in sexual frustration.

If I wasn't getting any, no reason for him to be, Lucy Lawless the Lawyer be damned.

There wasn't much to see in his bedroom, beyond the usual scattering of unnecessarily complex electronics: the bedside clock radio/CD player that projected a digital image of the time onto the ceiling, the TV and DVD player, the contraption that made soothing sounds from raindrops to surf to crickets, and that I assume he used for getting to sleep. If he used it at all. Scott had a love for gadgets, and the stores that sold them like Brookstone and The Sharper Image. He wasn't materialistic, he just liked the sheer gadgetry of the stuff. He'd once claimed it went with being a dentist.

His bed had no headboard, just a Hollywood frame under the boxsprings, and an uncovered ecru comforter on top of the sheets. There was one small Oriental carpet on the floor, and two framed museum posters of artworks by Klee on the walls that looked as if he'd had them since he'd been in college.

I wondered, if I opened the folding closet doors, if a pile of dirty clothes would tumble out. I was guessing yes.

The bathroom was similarly without interest, except for the ionic hair dryer, the electric nose and ear hair clipper, the Razor Care System and a CD player for the shower. The sink showed traces of soap and shaved whiskers. A basket of magazines sat by the toilet, holding back issues of *Men's Health* and *Bicycling,* a token issue of *The Smithsonian,* and a wrinkled *Victoria's Secret* catalog. I wondered which he actually looked at while in there.

Guys' bathrooms were so very different from women's. No jewelry in piles, no makeup, no bottles of lotions and hair products, no combs and clips, tweezers and nail scissors, curling iron and hot rollers with cords dangling and getting caught in the door. No matching bath rug and shower curtain, no half dozen shampoos and conditioners and bath gels and scrunchy body sponges. However did they groom themselves?

I was guessing, as with the closet, that if I pulled open a drawer in the cabinet I would find a treasure trove of shaving lotion, styptic pencils, aftershave, and probably more dental products than anyone could use in a year. And maybe that box of unused condoms. I nobly resisted the temptation to check, and to check for long hairs in a brush that might give away the lawyer's presence, and instead considered color schemes.

I was back in the living room, alternately contemplating the view of the darkening city and the possibilities of the room, if I were given my way and a platinum credit card, when Scott called me to dinner.

Dinner was pasta with a spicy red sauce, Caesar salad, kalamata olive bread and ice water with lemon.

"Pretty fancy," I said, impressed. "And here I was expecting hot dogs."

"Most of it was already made. You know, from the deli department at Zupan's."

"But it looks impressive. Better than the peanut butter and jelly I'd have had at home, if I was up to it."

"I was going to open a bottle of red wine, but..."

"I wouldn't have drunk any," I finished. He knew I wouldn't have anything to drink if I was going to drive. I have no head for alcohol.

We went to work on the food, chatting about possibilities for his duvet and pillows, and then the conversation wandered through work and eventually back to my perennial favorite, human relationships.

"The thing I don't get about this Pete guy," I said, "is how he could put so much effort into trying to get me into bed, then abandon the quest so quickly. I mean, I'd think I was worth a little more perseverance than that. Did he not like me at all? Was he just horny for an afternoon?"

"I thought you said the whole thing didn't bother you."

"It doesn't," I semi-lied. Pete didn't deserve to be made into a voodoo doll just yet. "I'm just trying to figure out the male mind."

"Don't look at me. I don't do that type of thing."

"Never?"

"The guy sounds like a jerk."

"But he was so cute."

Scott looked at me with raised brows.

"Maybe he just got busy," I said. "Maybe his ADHD kicked in, and he got distracted."

"And if he called, you'd go out with him again?" Scott asked in disbelief.

"Nooo..." I said.

"Hannah, you wouldn't, would you?"

"Maybe he had to go undercover and couldn't call."

"You said he was a patrol officer."

"Maybe he got shot."

"You should be so lucky." He made a noise of disgust. "I can't believe you'd go out with him again. He's already shown you what type of person he is."

"I know," I said. But I didn't know, and Scott knew it. "But maybe—"

"Maybe nothing," Scott interrupted. "For God's sake, you say you're trying to find a man to marry, a man who will treat you well and be a good father to your children, and here you are talking about spending time with a jerk-off like that. Why? Because he's 'cute'?"

"I didn't say I wanted to marry him," I said. "What's the matter, I can't have a little fun? Maybe all I want is sex, maybe that's the only reason I want to see him again. Guys do that all the time, why can't I?"

"If it was just about sex we wouldn't be talking about it. You could walk down the street and find a dozen guys willing to go to bed with you. You could have gone ahead and slept with this Pete, if that was what it was about."

"I thought about it."

"You're not like that. You don't sleep around."

"What is this, high school? The 1950's? No, I don't 'sleep around,' but not because of some outdated moral code. If I wasn't afraid of getting my heart broken or picking up some nasty disease, you can bet I'd take home anyone I felt like."

"Why don't you, then? Use protection. And if it's just one night, what risk is there of breaking your heart?" He sounded as upset as I felt. "If you're Miss Modern Values, why don't you act according to them?"

"Maybe I will," I said, as defiant as a teenager.

"You won't," he said, and in his voice was doubt, and the hope that I was lying.

"I don't know why it should matter to you, one way or another."

There was silence between us for a long moment. He poked at his cold noodles with his fork, then met my eyes. "I don't want to see you hurt. All I want for you is the best."

I had no answer for that. I almost said that it was for me to decide what *was* best, only I knew it would sound snotty. When someone is being noble and saying things for your best interest, it's too easy to come across like an ungrateful juvenile delinquent.

"Well, thanks," I finally muttered.

"You're welcome," he said, equally as gracious.

And we talked about other things.

Nineteen

Shoulder Pads and Falsies

Most of the next week went by in a confused blur of sewing, driving to appointments, playing on the Internet and reading the thrillers I'd picked up at the library.

Wonderful place, the library, where books and their accompanying escapism are free and ostensibly educational. If you eat to escape your moods, or shop, or have sex or drink, everyone says you have a problem. Read a book, and they think you're smart.

I had a nagging feeling of guilt and discomfort about the argument with Scott. We'd never argued quite like that before, never let our discussions get so personal, with feelings close to the surface.

The nagging feeling tinted my days gray, and I felt as though everything I said to my friends was wrong, felt that my interactions with customers were off, felt my sewing was not as good as it should have been, and the lack would be noted. And on top of the rest I felt puffy and bloated, my skin oily, new blemishes arising to give outward proof to the loser I was inside.

I knew the mood and accompanying loser-dom was temporary, I knew it was a matter of perception and that in a week or so all would be a sunny bright yellow again. But for now things were shadowy and incomplete, disjointed and murky with failure.

So I sewed and drove, read and ate and slept, and stayed up through the night looking at awful personal ads on the Internet, all in an attempt to not dwell on that argument with Scott. I had temporarily removed my own ad, knowing I was in too bitchy a state to answer any letters.

I didn't even work on my wedding dress. If I sewed it, he really *might* come, and I just couldn't be bothered to put on the makeup that would require.

Now it was Thursday, and I had an appointment with a new client, a pageant mother. She'd said on the phone she wanted me to make an evening gown and two other costumes for her twelve-year-old daughter, for a competition next month.

How could I possibly pass that up? It was almost as good as making wrestling costumes. Or maybe it was even better: kiddie pageants were surely the stranger, more perverted of the two.

The apartment complex where Carin Hoag lived was in the same part of town as Pete's, and of about the same price level, from the looks of it. I always wondered what it would have been like to have grown up calling a series of apartments home, instead of the house in Roseburg, where my room had always been my room, as if no one else could ever have lived there, or ever would in the future.

I suppose I would have adjusted, but still, I was glad that there was a specific place I could call home.

I parked, found the right door and knocked. I could

hear the tone of female voices sniping at each other, and waited. And waited a little longer, as the sniping continued. Then finally the door opened and I was facing a hard-faced girl who looked to be somewhere around eighteen or twenty. She had a burning cigarette wedged between two fingers.

A cigarette. Oh Lord. It seemed the only people in Oregon who smoked anymore were older people who hung out in bars playing the video poker machines, and the sort of teenagers who looked in need of social services before they ended up on heroin and giving blow-jobs for twenty bucks a head.

Everyone else was too busy hiking and shopping for organic vegetables.

"Yeah?" the creature asked, in way of greeting. She had on low-slung jeans tight enough to crease her crotch, and a form-fitting orange T-shirt that she must have bought in the children's department, it was so small. She took a professional suck on the cigarette, and I saw sore knees in her future.

"Ms. Hoag?" I asked.

The girl rolled her eyes. "That's my *mom.*"

"I'm Hannah O'Dowd. The seamstress?" I asked, trying to ring a bell in that sour head.

An older woman came down the short hall behind the girl, her hair frosted and teased, and covered with a fine cobwebbing of spray. She had parenthetical grooves around her mouth, and her magenta lipstick was bleeding into the fissures of her upper lip, despite the dark brown retaining wall of lip liner.

"You're going to ruin your skin, Bethany!" the

woman said, and snatched the cigarette from the girl's
fingers just as she was raising it again to her mouth.

This was Bethany? Twelve-year-old Bethany?

"You want me to get fat?" the girl snapped back.
"All the models smoke. Ballet dancers smoke. I'm going to get fat." She looked at me. "Bet you don't
smoke."

I weighed in my mind the likely five to seven hundred
dollars this job would gross, versus so much as ten
minutes in Bethany's company.

"Shut up," the elder Hoag said. Bethany tossed her
head and stomped off down the hall. "I'm sorry," Ms.
Hoag said. "She's angry because I won't let her go to
a rave tomorrow night. Please come in." She smiled in
what she probably thought was a warm, inviting manner,
but I felt as if I was being lured inside by a fairy-tale
witch, the type who can't quite hide the fact that the
oven is set to preheat.

The place smelled of sickly sweet floral air freshener
and cigarette smoke, and was furnished with cheap oak
tables and chairs, and a beige nubby-cloth couch above
which hung a framed print that looked as if it had come
straight off the furniture showroom floor. A fake plant
sat on top of the entertainment center, which was filled
with trophies and ribbons, as well as a TV and a shelf
of videotapes.

On the other walls hung picture after picture of Bethany in costume, crowns on her poofed head, ribbons
across her child's body. In the oldest photos she smiled
with baby teeth in a face made up like a refugee from
the eighties. I shuddered. Horror-flick monsters had
nothing on the creepiness of a child beauty queen.

Ms. Hoag saw me looking at the photos and gave me a rundown on each one. By the time we got to the end of them, I'd realized that Ms. Hoag had to have spent tens of thousands of dollars on costumes, entry fees, coaches and travel expenses, and in return she'd gotten the crappy faux trophies on the shelves and occasional prize money that might cover a night in a hotel.

I tried to think of a nice way to ask what was going through my mind, which was, "Why the hell are you wasting your money on this?" Instead, I asked, "So, uh, what drew you and Bethany to pageants?"

"It's an investment."

I raised my brows.

"At the higher levels, there's scholarship money up for grabs. I want Bethany to go to college, and this is how we're going to get the money." She took out a cigarette of her own and lit it. "I don't know how we could ever afford it otherwise."

The woman appeared oblivious that the funds for at least one college education had already been sucked down the drain of pageants. With idiot genes like that in her blood, I doubted Bethany would ever be seeing the doors of a hallowed institution, money or no.

The phone rang, and Bethany ran out of wherever she'd been sulking to get it, a rain of excited, squeaky chatter following. She carried the phone back into the depths of the apartment, yakking all the way.

Ms. Hoag took out one of the videotapes and shoved it into the VCR. "The gown I want made is on here," she said, as the image came up and she fast-forwarded through a home video of a pageant. "Do you have a VCR?"

"Yes."

"I'll give you the tapes to take home, with the costumes on them."

"You want me to copy one?" I had thought she wanted something original.

"Last year's winner. Here she is."

The tape stopped on a girl of unknown age, in an evening gown shimmering with beads and rhinestones, and the type of dangling, swaying excrescence on the shoulders that made me think of long-dead episodes of *Dynasty*. The girl looked strangely out of proportion, like a doll made to the wrong ratio of legs to body to head.

Her head with all its hair was nearly one-third of the girl's height, and looked as though it belonged on a twenty-year-old. Her body was as hip- and waist-less as an eight-year-old's, no matter what had to be falsies giving contour to her chest.

I began to feel sorry for Bethany. Then I decided it was better to feel sorry for myself, who would be spending hours making such a beastly costume.

I endured another half hour of videotape as Ms. Hoag found the other costumes she wanted, then she took me back to Bethany's room so I could take her measurements.

"I think Tyler's cuter than David," Bethany was saying on the phone. "He bumped into me in the hall. I know he did it on purpose. He's so immature! But I think he likes me." Then she saw us come in—Ms. Hoag still trailing cigarette smoke—whispered a goodbye, and shut off the phone.

"Muuu-ther!" Bethany said, rolling off the bed. "You know I don't let you smoke in my room."

"Hannah has to take your measurements," Ms. Hoag said. She purposefully took another drag on her cigarette, stared at her daughter, then left.

Bethany watched her go, then turned to me with a smirk. "I don't really smoke, you know. I just pretend, to piss her off. Maybe make her think about what she's doing to her own lungs and skin. Have you seen those wrinkles around her mouth?" Bethany asked, and gave a shudder. "God, this is all such a waste of time." She lifted her arms slightly to the side and stood still, in the pose of one waiting to be measured.

"Why do you still do it, then?" I asked, wrapping the tape measure around her and writing down the numbers in my notebook.

"Gives her something to do. She has no life."

Ah, an altruist. "You don't enjoy it at all?"

She shrugged. "It would be fun if I could choose my own outfits, or make up my own routines. Have you seen those tapes, have you seen the dumb-ass stuff they make us do? They should let us dance like on MTV."

She had a point of a sort, only I thought it would be even more disturbing to see pre-pubescent girls gyrating their hips than going through those stiff marionette motions on the tape.

"Your father...?" I asked.

"I'm going to see him in August. He's in Montana. They have horses up there—I wish I could live with him."

I finished with the measurements, but didn't want to stop talking to Bethany quite yet. She was kind of interesting. "Who's that Tyler guy you were talking about?"

She looked at me for a long moment, assessing. "You know, I was expecting you to be another of those middle-aged losers Mom hangs around with. You know the type, they all have Jesus sayings on their walls, and collect Beanie Babies, as if that was not so over. You're not like them, though."

"Heaven forbid."

"So can I ask you something?"

"Sure," I said.

"What *is* it with guys?"

"Hey, I'm still trying to figure that one out myself."

"I mean, why is it the only way they can show they like you, is by being mean to you?" she asked, hand on hip.

"They grow out of that. At least, most of them do."

She didn't look satisfied with that answer. I sat on the edge of her bed, and tried to remember when I had been twelve years old. Had I known *anything* back then? No, and I doubted, for all her airs, that Bethany knew anything, either.

"Listen," I said. "You want to know what I wish someone had told me about boys when I was twelve?"

"Sure."

Of course she did. And whatever I said, I knew it wouldn't make a difference. As with most things, you had to learn it on your own.

"Okay. Most boys only start acting like adults when they reach their late twenties. If then. So, you've got at least fifteen years ahead of you during which to build your own life, without fussing over any idiot boys."

"What, not date?" she asked in disbelief.

"No, you've got to date, to practice dealing with them. And it can be fun. I just mean, put yourself first. Don't put aside what you want to do for the sake of a boy."

"Not even for love?"

"Why love a guy who doesn't want you to pursue your own goals and interests? What type of jerk is that?"

She shrugged, obviously not satisfied with my words of wisdom. "Any other advice?"

I smiled, and stood. "Just the usual, that you've heard before. There are always more fish in the sea. Keep your friends. They'll be there after the boy is gone. Wait until you're older to have sex, and then always use a condom. Wait to get married."

She rolled her eyes.

"Yeah, I know," I said. "But I meant what I said. The boys will come and go. You're the only one who will be with you your whole life, so treat yourself well. Treat yourself...with all the devotion you'd give a boy you were in love with."

"Is that what you do?"

"Hey, I'm still learning this stuff. I'm just trying to give you the benefit of my suffering."

"Huh." She looked doubtful.

I looked at my watch, seeking an excuse to end this conversation before I gave myself away as a hypocrite. "Jeez, I gotta go," I said.

I went and found Ms. Hoag, and collected the tapes. I promised to call her with an estimate on price and time, and left. I had just gotten in my car when my cell phone rang.

"Hannah's Custom Sewing."

"Hannah? Pete, here. You ready for that hike?"

Twenty

Latex

He had a truly beautiful butt.

They say that women hit their sexual peak in their late thirties. I was still a couple months from even being *in* my thirties, and already I was turning into a guy, the way I was salivating over a beautiful butt. What would happen at thirty-five? Thirty-nine? Would they have to take a fire hose to me? Would I be attacking college guys? Would I be the type of older woman that mothers never thought to warn their boys about?

"You doing okay?" Pete asked, turning around to check on me. We were an hour into a hike up a trail in the Mt. Hood National Wilderness, and the whole time had been climbing switchbacks under the deep shade of conifers. I was ready for a break, and could happily spend it kneading his butt.

"I think I need some water." Then, baby, let's hit the bushes. Rrrar! I considered how much more enjoyable this exercise business would be if he would take off his shirt.

"I could do with some, too," he said, stopping.

I took off my small backpack and retrieved my water

bottle. Pete had his slung on an athletic-looking contraption of neoprene and netting, that had been nestling
atop his spine.

A middle-aged couple went by, going the opposite
direction, smiling and saying hello, swinging their hiking sticks. We smiled and greeted back.

It was Tuesday, so we had been hoping to have the
trail largely to ourselves, but it was also a lovely day
and Portland is filled with outdoors enthusiasts. Still, the
fellow hikers were nothing compared to what they
would be on the weekend.

I didn't know if it had been horniness, lack of self-
respect, or curiosity that had impelled me to accept
Pete's invitation. On the phone he had seemed completely unaware that I might have taken it wrong that he
hadn't called for two weeks. He'd explained his long
silence as "work" and "I had to help a buddy move on
my days off."

With Scott's admonishments burning in my brain, I'd
gone ahead and accepted. Maybe I was doing it to prove
I made my own decisions, and that I could be a wild
thing if I wanted.

Besides, I had to get my money's worth out of those
hiking boots. And when was I ever again going to get
so close to such a gorgeous piece of meat?

Yeah, all right, a five-year-old had better powers of
concentration and more interesting things to say than
Pete the Big-Talking Cop, but...

Once in her life a girl just had to be naughty.

And maybe he really did like me, and maybe there
was a tiny chance that the backyard barbecue future was
possible.

And maybe I just wanted to see him naked. It had to have been the newness of being with him, that had kept me from reacting with more excitement when we'd been making out in his apartment. Today, with a couple more hours together, the old hormones should be firing up like the engines on the space shuttle.

One would think.

The water in my bottle was warm and tasted plasticky, but still my heat-sensitive tooth cringed. I grimaced and put the bottle back in my pack, and we resumed our trudge through the splendors of the wilderness, Pete starting in on a story about pulling over a drunk driver who'd been swerving all over the road, his equally wasted girlfriend in the passenger seat.

"So I asked him where he was going, and you know what the idiot said? 'I'm going to get lucky!' The girlfriend kept trying to get him to shut up, but he was too interested in being a smart-ass."

The stories were starting to blend together, and I'd already realized that each had the same ending: Pete, through his cleverness and bravery, catching the dirt bag and making the world a better place. He had a sort of jumpy, tense energy to him while he talked, as if remembering the confrontations brought on a surge of adrenaline. It was wearying to listen to.

I made the appropriate sounds of interest while he displayed his macho worthiness, and focused on making it another hundred yards without stopping. I was concerned just how musky my panties were going to be by the end of this hike. It is a worry, when one has hopes of oral sex.

The trail wound through both meadow and forest, and

across small, swift rivers. After another hour and a half we finally reached our goal: a waterfall.

It didn't have the height of the falls in the Columbia Gorge, or the power of those at Silver Falls State Park, but I was so glad to know we were done climbing I didn't care. The falling water created a cool, misty breeze, and I stood at the edge of the rocky pool and soaked it in.

"Awesome, isn't it?" Pete asked.

I murmured a positive sound, and opened my eyes, looking around the small clearing. There was a man with a camera and a tripod, and two older women who were leaving. "Shall we eat here?" There were energy bars in my pack. The hiking had killed my hunger, but I'd take any excuse to prolong our rest before beginning the descent back through the forest.

"I know a place upstream a bit, it's quiet, it's a nice spot. We could put our feet in the water."

"How far upstream?" I asked, and wondered how many women he'd taken up here. I wasn't afraid I'd end up a corpse buried under a rotting log, but neither was I too fond of the idea of being another proverbial notch on the old standard-issue gunbelt. I was here to take advantage of *his* lovely body, not the other way around.

"Not far, five or ten minutes," he said.

"Okay." Why not?

We had to go around the falls, climbing again, and this time not on a real trail. I suspected the Park Service would disapprove of the destruction our boots were wreaking on tender plant life, but was too wimpy to point it out to Mr. Upholder of the Law.

Another fifteen minutes, and I was glad enough I'd

been quiet: we came out at a stretch of gurgling stream dappled in sunlight, the banks shaded, rocks and boulders covered in green moss, and not another soul in sight. I dropped down onto the sandy-dirt bank and went to work on my boots.

Pete dropped down beside me and did the same. "I dare you to skinny-dip," he said.

I peeled off my socks, my feet imprinted in pink with their texture. "I dare *you*," I said, ever so wittily.

"I will, if you do," he said, with what he probably thought was a rakish grin.

There wasn't much question about where this would lead, if I accepted, and I had the necessary supplies for such a conclusion in my backpack. A scout should always be prepared.

But I hesitated. Did I really want to do it? Maybe I was only tempted because I wanted to prove I wasn't bound by outdated morals.

On the other hand, it might truly be fun.

And there wasn't any real reason not to.

I grinned at him, a what-the-hell smile, and took off my shirt, then with a quick turn of the arm reached back and unhooked my bra.

"Hot damn!" he said, and then tore off his own shirt.

I stripped and stood, and realized I was buck naked in the middle of the forest. I kind of liked it. Buck naked in a shopping mall, no, but out here…it was almost like being a beast of the wild.

Pete threw off his underpants and stood, and after a quick glance at the goods—too quick to get a sense of what he had to offer—I trotted the few steps to the stream and pranced into the water.

And pranced right back out again.

"Good Lord! It's freezing!"

"What did you expect? It's coming off the mountain," he said, all manly knowledge. I'd bet Wade stood a better chance of surviving out here for a week than Pete.

He splashed into the stream, and as he passed my eye strayed to the bit of darker flesh that bounced and bobbed on its bed of hairy balls. I wasn't sure, but he might not be circumcised. That would be a first for me, and had the potential of fun, if he'd let me play with the foreskin.

He made his way to the middle of the stream, arms out for balance as he found his footing on the smooth stones, legs and buttocks flexing like an exhibit at an anatomy lecture. The water was only shin-deep.

"How are we supposed to swim in that?" I asked, arms crossed over my breasts. I wished I had a video camera. This was better than a Sasquatch sighting. It was better, I suspected, than those movies at The Purple Palace.

"You weren't intending on doing the crawl, were you?" he asked, turning so that he faced downstream, the water pushing up the backs of his calves. And then he sat, all at once. "Wooo-hoo!" he cried. "Christ! Wooo-oo-oo!"

Any hiker within a half mile could hear him.

"Wooooo! Damn, it's cold!" With his hands he splashed water up onto his face and chest, and under his arms. He quickly lay back, dunking his head under, then came up howling and shouting.

"Pete! For God's sake, you're going to draw someone right to us."

"Nah, they won't want anything to do with us. Come on! Get in! Wooo!"

I had started to cool down from the hike, and the water was even less inviting now than it had been a couple minutes ago. I bit my lip, and looked at Pete, and then he held his arms open to me.

Well, hell, *that* would keep me warm.

I clenched my fists and forced myself into the water, making my slow way to Pete, my eyes on the muscled, sunlight-dappled prize. My foot slipped on a stone and I lost my balance, catching it just before a facer in the water, but now I was bent over, one hand on the creek bottom.

Fabulous. So flattering, to have one's rump in the air, and breasts hanging free of support like a pair of mangoes ready to drop.

Pete didn't seem to mind, though, and behaved like a typical boy: he splashed me.

"Hey!"

"Come on, you wuss! Get over here!"

I thought of Bethany, and the years of such behavior she had yet to endure. Wasn't I too old for this?

He splashed me again, and I thought, *The hell with it,* and lunged the last several feet, falling onto him, knocking us both full length into the water.

"Yai!" I cried, coming up, wiping water and hair off my face. Pete had me in his arms, sprawled cross-wise across his lap as the water beat against us like jets in a spa.

"It's great!" he said.

His body was a little warmer than the water, the broadness of his back shielding me from much of the force of the stream. I liked the feel of our naked skin together, the contact sometimes smooth, sometimes juddering like a windshield wiper with too little rain.

I wrapped my arm around his neck, and he got the hint and kissed me, one of his hands going down to play with my cold, shriveled breast.

And like the day in his apartment, I felt nothing.

Physically he was doing well enough, his tongue playing with mine without being sloppy, his hand a little rough but not utterly without skill, and his toned body was everything I could wish for.

And yet...

Inside, there was no excitement. I was going through the motions.

His hand slipped down between my legs, and I spread them. Maybe it would help get my fires burning. His fingers played and stroked, and I held him close, moving my mouth to his neck, sucking there and acting as if he was getting me going.

Maybe the cold water had numbed my crotch.

"Shall we take this to dry ground?" I asked in a fake sultry whisper.

He shifted position, and then stood, lifting me in his arms and carrying me back to the bank, water dripping off us. Now *this* was nice. I felt so wonderfully small and feminine being carried by a guy, as long as he was strong enough to do so without grunting, and his muscles betrayed no quiver of effort. It's not flattering to have a guy straining under your weight.

Wild man of the forest, I am yours!

Back on the bank we arranged our discarded clothes into a ground cover, and I lay back and let Pete kiss his way down my breasts and belly. He was approaching Pleasure Central when I stopped him by digging my fingers into his hair.

"There's, uh...nothing I need to know about, is there?" I asked, before he could lay his mucous membranes against my own.

"Huh?"

I widened my eyes at him, urging him to understand. "You know. Health-wise. Any problems?"

"Oh. No. Got tested for HIV, I'm clean."

"So am I," I said, although what I really wanted to do was ask, "No papilloma virus? No herpes? Been with anyone with chlamydia lately?" But it didn't seem polite to prolong the questioning. He surely would have told me then if there was something else. Wouldn't he?

I wondered if he would have asked me the same question, if I had not brought it up first?

Had he asked *any* of the women he'd been with? Maybe he didn't know what he'd picked up from them. Maybe he was a swarming mass of viruses, all waiting to leap into my pristine body and multiply, guaranteeing that for the rest of my life I would have to have "the talk" with every guy I wanted to sleep with.

Then he went down, and I decided I'd done the minimum required of a responsible young woman.

His tongue was warm against my chilled flesh, and I waited for the magic to take me over. I'd never known oral sex to not eventually get me where I wanted to go.

He settled down between my legs, his arms going under my thighs and his hands coming round to rest on my hip bones. I bent my knees up and let my legs fall to the side, opening myself like a butterfly.

I stared up at the dark boughs of the firs, and the scatterings of blue sky. A crow cawed. The river burbled. It was all very lovely, and why wasn't Pete hitting the right spot? What was he doing over in that dull valley, instead of in the gold rush ravine?

Come on, man, work it!

His tongue went all over the place, hitting only by occasional chance on the motherlode.

Should I tell him? Gently guide him? Guys didn't seem to appreciate having the bull's-eye pointed out to them, at least not the way I did it. "Hannah, you make me feel like I'm just a machine for your pleasure," one had complained. "It's like I could be anyone, as long as I did what you wanted."

Whine, whine, whine. Too bad I didn't have one of those sixteen-inch elephant clits.

Oh, yes, there! Yes! Yes!

Dammit. Gone again.

How long was it going to take to walk back down to the trail head? Hope my knees could take it. The car's probably hot. Hope no one has broken into it. And why couldn't Pete have driven? Yeah, I have air conditioning, but I'd go for open windows, if it meant not having to drive for a change.

"Is it good?" Pete asked, peeking up from the depths.

"Oh, yeah." Ah, crap. Why couldn't I tell him where to go? There was my chance, gone now.

Yes! Yes! He found it! He was there!

Gone.

Maybe he was doing it on purpose, taunting me.

Nah. He struck me more as the get-her-ready-so-you-can-pork-her type. Speed would be a virtue. Still, he was trying, and I wasn't likely to get this type of attention again anytime soon, so I'd better make the best of it.

I was out in the forest, and had been captured by savage wild men. Yes! They have never had a real woman, but all have been trained on a stone model in how to please her. They are holding my arms and legs down, and taking turns giving me pleasure.

Yes!

Only, a stone model is not the same as a real woman, so they make mistakes. But they are hungry for me. It is the highest honor in their society, to bring an orgasm to a woman. They will fight for the chance!

Yes!

This one is trying so hard, trying to get me there before his brethren pull him away to have their own chance. His tongue is moving so quickly, so fiercely, and there! He hits the spot.

I'm growing attached to him. I want him to succeed. Quick, hit it again! I'll come for you, my hairy friend. Try! Try!

"You're wet and ready for me," Pete said, rising up.

No! No! Not yet! I want more! Or maybe I'll get there with a little more solid action.

Pete lay down beside me, and brought my hand to Mr. Weenie, who needed a little attention before he was going to be ready for the Great Thrust. I stroked and fondled, and tried to hold on to the fading excitement of my fantasy. He stiffened up, and Pete started to roll on top of me.

"I've got stuff in my pack," I said, meaning condoms, et cetera.

"I'll be careful, we can go without."

"Uh, no. I'd really rather use something."

He sighed, and rolled off me. "Fine. I have my own."

I raised my brows. "Feeling cocky, were you?"

"Hey, a guy has to hope. And it's not like you weren't thinking the same thing." He reached over to his small bag and dug around in one of the small zippered pockets. Meanwhile I reached for my own pack and dragged it over.

"Er, there's something I need to do, too," I said. "Would you mind not watching?"

He shrugged and turned away, busying himself with tearing open a packet that I hoped hadn't been in that bag for too many months. Unlikely, given what I guessed about his sexual habits.

I took a box of spermicide out of my pack, opened it, and tore the end off one of the long, thin plastic tubes. I lay back and inserted it, feeling as if I was performing a gynecological procedure on myself. Where was the slide, upon which to smear the sample?

I squeezed the plastic reservoir between my fingers, and with an internal squirt the sperm killer was successfully delivered. Hurrah for science!

But was one dose really enough?

Of course I'd read the box and instructions, but it just didn't seem sufficient. The last time I'd had sex, I'd been in a monogamous relationship and on the pill. Rubbers and potions just didn't seem as reliable. And what if Pete did have nasty critters? The more Nonoxynol-9, the better, in my estimation.

What the hell. I took another tube out of the box and sent the contents up where they belonged. He'd probably just think I was creaming myself for him.

I stuffed the empty tubes back in the box and put it in my pack, then lay back down, trying to recapture the moment.

The hairy wild man loses control of himself, his friends try to pull him away, but he must have me! He must! He is breaking the final taboo of the tribe, and trying to pork me: his weenie cannot wait.

What was taking him so long?

"I hate these things," he said, coming back and positioning himself over me, braced on his arms.

"My wild man. Take me!" And stop whining about the damn condom.

He reached down and fiddled with himself, with those jerking motions a girl knows mean that he is coaxing the blood back into the little feller. It was a tad insulting that he felt the need to do it, when I was lying here in all my natural glory.

I put my hands on his shoulders, stroking them, and stroking down his chest. He did have beautiful shoulders, and a chest deserving of lascivious touches. I put my hands over his pecs and squeezed, like a guy feeling out a girl's breasts.

"What are you doing?"

"I could just eat you up," I said.

He laughed under his breath, then at last sent the sailor home to port.

Ow. "Ooo, go slow, can you?" I said softly, trying not to grimace.

How long had it been since I'd had sex? Things had

closed up since then. He felt a hell of a lot bigger than he had looked.

I reached down and felt around him, fingers sliding over latex, confirming that he was as middling-size as I recalled. No elephants or donkeys here, thank God.

"Relax, baby," he said.

Shut up, you bonehead. "I'm trying. You're so *big*," I said. That ought to make him happy.

"Let me in, honey. Let me take you to the moon."

Was he serious? "Shh…" I said as gently as I could, and gave a sultry smile. If he kept quiet maybe I could return to the wild man fantasy.

I closed my eyes. Wild man is aching to enter, even having his tip inside me is more pleasure than he's ever known….

A few more minutes, and Pete was inside, stroking away, and thanks to my mental wild man I was almost enjoying myself.

Then he slipped out, and fumbled getting it back in, jabbing me with the blunt end. A couple more stabs and then he was back in place…or at least, I thought he was back in place. Or was he just pounding his hips against me?

It is never polite to ask, "Are you in yet?"

A moment later he was definitely out, and he made me turn over and go up on all fours. He reentered— although I couldn't be sure—had he shrunk?—and went back to work. I stared out at the trees, and considered how very like a creature on one of those wildlife shows I felt. The female always looked rather bored, while the male went at his business behind her.

If I were a praying mantis, I could tear his head off and eat it.

I closed my eyes again and brought back the wild man. He grunts and strains. His companions are getting excited, their hands going to their own weenies. They feel themselves ready to come.

Pete's stroking slowed, his movements uncertain, then stopping altogether.

"What?" I asked.

"I don't know. Something..."

Then suddenly he pulled out, the suction making a loud and uncomfortable plurp! in my nether regions. "Hey!" I complained.

"What have you got in there?" he asked, his voice rising.

"Got in where?"

"What did you put up your snatch?" he screeched.

I turned around. He was holding his weenie in his hand, staring at it.

"Where's the condom?" I asked, feeling my throat tighten. Had he left it inside? Did he think vagina gremlins had pulled it off?

"I took it off."

"What! When?"

"Did you put spermicide up there? Is that what you did?" he asked.

"Yes, of course."

"Shit! I thought you were putting in a diaphragm. Fuck!"

"What did you do?" I screeched, getting as upset as he was. "Where's the condom?"

"I told you, I took it off! I couldn't feel a thing through it, so when you turned around I took it off!"

"You *what?*"

"It's not important. My dick, look at my dick! My God, how much of that crap did you use?"

I looked at the organ in question. Indeed, it did not look well. The opening at the end was crimson, and the rest had an unusually vibrant rosy glow. He was indeed uncircumcised, the foreskin pulled back from the head like a scrunched-down turtleneck. He probably wasn't going to let me play with it now.

"Huh," I said helpfully.

"It stings. God, it stings." He stood and went to the river and washed it off, then stood, holding it between his fingertips, a grimace on his face.

"What? What are you doing?"

"Trying to take a piss. The stuff has gone up inside, I have to get it out."

"You shouldn't have taken off the condom," I said. Served the bastard right. Who did he think he was, taking it off without my permission?

"Aaaaa!" he cried as a spurt of urine came out.

Good. Let him scream.

"Aaaaa! Shit! God damn! Fuck!"

Good thing I'd used a double dose. Who knows what was crawling around that penis, if he never used a condom? I would never have known he'd taken it off, either, if I hadn't used so much.

The more I thought about it, the angrier I got. Who was he to make decisions about my health without consulting me? Who was he to assume anything about what I'd put up there? *He* wasn't the one who would have to bear the consequences of a pregnancy or passing on a disease.

"Aaaaa!"

Hikers for half a mile probably thought there was a mountain lion screaming. He was making an awful lot of noise.

"You should have left it on," I said again. I squatted down by the water and washed myself off, feeling quite fond of spermicide.

And none too fond of Pete.

Twenty-One

Wet Terry Cloth

"So the moral of the story is to always booby-trap one's vagina," I said.

"That is just wrong, what he did," Louise said, standing beside her stove with one hand on her hip and the other holding a spatula.

The smell of garlic was heavy and delicious in the air. Louise was making seafood fettucine, and I'd already taken a peek at the tiramisu that was for dessert. A girl could have worse friends than one who loved to cook, and loved best of all to cook for others.

I sipped a diet soda, sitting at her small kitchen table, already set for two.

"Maybe he learned a lesson," I said. "If he's not afraid of disease or of getting a girl pregnant, maybe he'll at least be wary of hurting his weenie from now on."

"I just don't get guys. I mean, what if he did get a girl pregnant?"

"He'd probably offer to go fifty-fifty on the abortion."

Louise snorted, and stirred the garlic in the pan. "And

if she didn't want one? Guys are so stupid. She could have the baby, then sue him for paternity. He'd be paying child support for the next twenty years.''

I pulled my foot up onto the seat of my chair, and crossed my arms on top of my knee. ''He didn't strike me as a 'think before you act' type of guy. The ADHD, you know.''

''What a freakin' excuse. He was just a jerk, and the ADHD had nothing to do with it.''

''You know, with all the women out there who are hungry for babies, I'd think guys would be a lot more cautious. I could see a woman choosing a guy with a steady income, taking him home, then saying, 'You don't want to wear a condom? Sure! No problem!' Then she gets pregnant, and has a guaranteed supplemental income to help her raise the child, without the bother of a husband.''

''You're twisted.''

''Ten minutes of selfish, it-feels-better-without-a-rubber sex, and he's not only a sperm donor, he's having his wages garnished. Maybe if I get desperate enough...''

''You wouldn't,'' Louise said.

''No, I wouldn't.''

''Thanks again for Voodoo Derek, by the way. You're right, it's therapeutic to zap him with rubber bands.''

''I'm glad to have been of service.'' Voodoo Derek had a tiny eyeless head to symbolize his idiocy and blindness, and a penis with an unhappy face at the end, a symbol of what he would not be getting from Louise.

''Are you going to make a Voodoo Pete?'' she asked.

"Of course—" I started to say, and was distracted by the faint ringing of my cell phone. "Botheration," I said, and went to the living room to dig it out of my purse.

"Hannah's Custom Sewing," I said.

"Hannah?" Dad asked, his voice tight.

"Dad?" I said, the tone of his voice enough to send a lance through my heart.

"Hannah, your mother's in the hospital. Can you come down here?"

"Dad! What happened?" My heart was pounding.

"She's had a stroke." His voice broke, and it was several seconds before he could speak again. "I found her in the bathroom. They did some sort of scan, they've given her something to dissolve the clot, now we're waiting for her to wake up."

"Is she going to be okay?" I asked. I was still standing, I was still breathing. I was all right, I was coping, the news hadn't flattened me.

"They don't know yet. They won't know until she wakes up."

"I'll come right now. You're at Mercy?"

"Yes."

We said goodbye, and I stood there with the phone in my hand, still floating somewhere above reality, my mind racing. Did I need to stop back at the house to get anything? No, I had my purse, I could buy whatever I needed down there. My car was parked on the street: five minutes from the curb I could be at the entrance to I-5 southbound, if I pushed it I could make the trip in two and a half hours—

"Hannah?" Louise asked from the kitchen doorway,

her voice telling me she knew something was wrong. "What happened?"

I turned to her. "My mom had a stroke," I said, and as I said the words the reality of it hit me, consideration of toothbrushes and sleepwear and gas in the car giving way to Mom in the hospital, maybe dying, maybe never to recover, maybe never to be the same as she had been.

I may have lost my mom.

The muscles of my face pulled back in a grimace of grief, tears filling my eyes. "She's in the hospital. They're waiting for her to wake up."

I couldn't breathe, my breath held on a sob, the tears spilling down, my face and throat aching from the strain.

"Oh, honey," Louise said, and came and held me. I lay my head against her shoulder and wept, snuffling and dripping.

"I'm getting you wet," I said after a few minutes, pulling back and wiping at my nose with my wrist. Grief was being washed over by something akin to panic, and the need to get down to Roseburg as quickly as possible. And Dad, poor Dad, how was he coping?

"Like it matters. Go grab the box of Kleenex from the bathroom. I'm driving you down there."

"I can drive myself."

"No, you can't. Go get the Kleenex."

I did as she bade, and in the bathroom looked at myself in the mirror as I thought again about Mom, and if she would ever be the same. The fear and the grief returned, and my face twisted, my mouth pulling down like a tragic Greek mask, a high-pitched keening sound in the back of my throat.

The clothes I wore, the cut of my hair, the studs in

my ears, they were all useless decoration, incongruously stuck to a mass of pain. Nothing mattered, but that my mom was sick. I could be wearing real diamonds, I could have my own house and drive a Jaguar, I could be beautiful and brilliant and famous, and it would mean nothing.

Nothing mattered, but that I might lose my mom.

The wave of pain receded, and I wet a washcloth and cleaned the smeared mascara off my face. I grabbed the Kleenex box, knowing the wave would come again, and when I came back out to the living room Louise had her jacket and mine, and ushered me out the door.

"I can't leave my car on the street," I said.

"We'll take it."

"How will you get home?" I asked.

"Don't worry about that."

I wanted to drive myself, for the distraction, but Louise wouldn't allow it. So I settled myself into the passenger seat, and experienced the horror of having someone else at the wheel of my car. It was a better distraction than driving myself ever could have been.

Twenty-Two

Blue Medallion Print

I sat beside Dad, the both of us in chairs at the side of Mom's bed. The embolism had been in her left hemisphere, according to the CT scan, so it was her right side that might not function when she awoke. We sat on her left side, Dad holding her hand, wanting to be sure that she could feel that he was there.

It was two o'clock in the morning, and the intensive care unit had a quiet, half-lit feel to it, strangely peaceful. Hospitals had never frightened me, I'd always thought of them as "home base" for the injured. If you made it there, you were safe. You would be taken care of. Someone would fix you.

It was a bit of a shock to discover that there was very little anyone could do to "fix" a stroke. They had given Mom an anticoagulant, they had given her a blood thinner, and that was the extent of what they could do. They could not go in and fix whatever damage had been done to her brain, they could not force her to wake up, they could not make it impossible for her to have another stroke in the future.

We were helpless. If there had been anything to do,

I would have done it, but all there was was waiting. Mom had to emerge on her own.

I looked at her face, slack and unconscious above the hospital gown with its blue medallion print. I wondered what her reaction would be when she awoke and understood what had happened to her. If she *could* understand. She might not be able to read. She might not be able to talk. Would she want to live?

I wanted her to die instantly, right now, and avoid any suffering, and free me from the pain of watching her suffer. And at the same time, I wanted her to live, to drag herself through any misery, just so I wouldn't have to give her up. She could be silent, wheelchair-bound, helpless, and the spark of life within her would still be Mom. And I would not be alone.

"You should go lie down for a bit," Dad said, startling me out of my thoughts.

"No, I'm fine."

"Go on. Louise is probably still in the waiting room. Go get something to drink, or something to eat. I'll stay with her, as long as they'll let me."

"Okay." I didn't want to go, but I wanted to argue even less, and I thought maybe Dad would feel he was doing something if he could at least be sure that I was being properly fed and rested. "I'll be out in the waiting room, if you need me."

He nodded, not looking at me, his eyes on Mom.

I went down the hall and through the doors to the waiting room outside the intensive care unit. It was a quiet room, the carpeting and padded furniture muffling any sound that distressed family members might make. Magazines were spread across a coffee table, and through a doorway could be seen a small room full of humming vending machines.

Louise and Scott were sitting on one of the couches, the table lamp beside Louise casting golden light on her brown curls. She must have called him soon after we arrived, when I first went in to see Mom. The staff only let us stay with her for short periods of time.

Louise looked as though she belonged next to Scott, with his own dark hair and his perfect chin. They could have been brother and sister; or husband and wife—one of those pairs who grow to look like one another. I had a fleeting thought that maybe someday, despite Louise's protestations to the contrary, they might get back together again.

"Hannah," Louise said, seeing me and standing.

Scott turned and saw me, then stood and came and folded me in his arms. "I'm so sorry," he said into my hair.

I remembered then that Scott's father had died of a heart attack several years ago. He had been through worse than what I was going through, and he would understand. I wrapped my arms around him and hugged back, closing my eyes and for a precious few moments letting myself feel nothing but the comfort of human closeness. I leaned against him, and did not try to be strong.

I had cried in Louise's arms because I could not help it. With Scott, I did not feel the need to help it. It had always been that way with me, with boyfriends. I felt no need to pretend to be strong, to put on a brave face with a guy I was close to: it was his job to be the strong one. I was supposed to burden him with my troubles.

But Scott wasn't my boyfriend. I pulled away, and he let me go, although I wanted nothing more than to fall asleep in those warm arms, snuggled close where I could pretend that nothing could hurt me and no bad thoughts could follow.

"Any change?" Scott asked.

"No."

"I got a hold of Cass at the pub. She's probably on her way already, with some of your things," Louise said.

"She doesn't have to do that," I protested by rote, but the truth was I was touched the three of them cared enough to come all the way down here for me. I sniffed back an encroaching tear.

"Nonsense," Louise said.

"I've brought you a toothbrush and paste," Scott said. "And floss, of course."

My mouth crooked in a smile, despite my mood. "You would."

"There's also some bottled juices in the cooler," he said, nodding toward the end of the couch, where a small blue chest was sitting. "I know you won't feel much like eating anything, so we have to get the vitamins in you somehow."

"Thanks."

Louise dragged the little chest around to the front of the couch and opened it, taking out a couple bottles and putting them on the coffee table. "I'm going to go dash to the ladies' room," she said, "and go see if there's a snack bar open. I don't trust the sandwiches in those machines. You okay?"

I nodded, and went and sat on the couch. Scott came

and sat next to me, opening a bottle of juice and handing it to me. I took a sip, then rested it against my thigh, staring into space.

Scott took my free hand, and held it clasped gently in his own in the space between us on the couch. "Whatever happens, Hannah," he said, "you'll never be alone."

And the tears started again.

"Hannah, wake up." It was Dad's voice, his hand on my shoulder, stirring me from sleep. I opened my eyes, squinting against the daylight bright in the wall of windows that had been dark a few hours earlier. I had Scott's cotton handkerchief wadded in my hand, almost dry now.

"What is it? What's happened?" I asked. I'd been napping on one of the couches in the waiting area. Louise and Scott were gone, Cassie asleep on the other couch in their place, a bag of my clothes and toiletries on the floor.

"She's awake!"

"She is? How is she?" I asked, sitting up and throwing off the jacket that had been serving as my blanket.

"The doctor is in with her now, but she recognized me, she could say my name. That's supposed to be good, if she can speak."

"Can I go in? Can I see her?"

"Come on."

We went back to the room together, standing out of the doctor's way as he finished checking Mom. He saw us and motioned us forward, smiling.

"You've been lucky, Mrs. O'Dowd," he said to

Mom, although plainly speaking to us, as well. "You were unconscious for only twelve hours. You can move your right arm and leg a little, and this is a very good sign. Your speech and movements are going to be slow, but they will become faster with time and therapy."

I took in his words, the caution mixed with optimism, the absence of the words "full recovery," but what mattered was that Mom had a weak smile and was looking at me and at Dad, and even as the doctor kept talking I went to the bed and bent down, putting my cheek to hers and then giving her a kiss.

"You...have...b-b-black...under...your eyes," Mom said as I pulled away.

I smiled, and rubbed at my skin. The washcloth at Louise's hadn't removed all of it. "Mascara. I didn't wash my face last night."

"B-b-bad...for...your skin."

"I know. I need to take a shower."

"Yes."

Dad came to the other side of the bed and took her hand, and she turned her attention to him. He made a suspicious sound, and when I looked at his face I saw he was weeping, trying to hold it back, trying to hide it, but the tears were spilling down his cheeks.

I wanted to stay, but at the same time this was too private for that. My parents were not ones to express love for each other openly, and this was more bare and raw than I knew what to do with. I crept from the room, the doctor already on his way out, but still I heard Dad.

"I thought I'd lost you."

I didn't know where either of us would be, without her.

Twenty-Three

Old Denim

I lay in my old bed, in my old room, and gave up on trying to sleep. It was 1:00 a.m., the house was quiet, the night sounds of crickets through my open window soothing, but sleep was not coming.

Tomorrow Mom would be coming home.

It had been three weeks since her stroke. After she'd awakened, she'd been moved to a regular ward room, and had gone daily to the physical therapy center at the hospital. The doctor now said there was no reason for her to stay in the hospital: she would do fine at home, and would come in for physical therapy several times a week. A home health nurse would make visits to the house for as long as needed.

The three weeks had felt like three months, from the confusion and busy days. I'd been splitting my time between home and Portland, trying to keep Mom and Dad's house in order, to see Mom for a couple hours, and to keep my business going.

I'd ended up carting my sewing machine along with me most nights I came down, and sewing at the house until I couldn't stay awake any longer, whereupon I'd fall into bed, sleeping without dreams until my alarm went off and I began the mad dash all over again. Most of my clients were understanding of my situation, but I worried that along with the understanding they might decide to relieve me of the burden of their patronage.

I felt shallow for even worrying about it, but there it was, and here I was awake in the middle of the night, considering the possibility that I might have to move home.

As much as he loved Mom, how could Dad possibly take care of her? He couldn't run the VCR correctly; he needed help making a cheese sandwich; he couldn't be trusted to pick something up at the grocery store, for fear he'd see a five gallon jar of pickles on sale, or a vat of peanut butter it would take a large family three years to eat. Mom ordered his blood pressure medication, she bought his clothes, she fed him, she kept the house. Who was going to take over all that needed to be done, and insure that Mom got what she needed?

Who was there but me?

And I wanted to do it, I wanted to make sure Mom got all that she needed. If I wasn't here, I would be worried that Dad wasn't doing what he should—not through laziness on his part, but ignorance and incompetence.

And yet, at the same time, there was part of me that was afraid of what the future might look like, if I moved home.

I might never leave again.

Mom might have another stroke. Dad might fall ill. And I would be the spinster daughter, the caretaker, who is duty-bound to care for her parents for one year, for two, for three, for ten, her own life passing her by while she cared for others.

I had read about such characters in books, and seen them in movies. They were women who grew fat and shy, entombed in the house, only emerging back into the world in their late forties, like groundhogs coming out of their den and seeing the sun, all squinty-eyed and scared.

I would do it, because I loved my parents too much not to.

And I would resent my role, because I wanted my freedom.

I turned on the bedside lamp and got out of bed, heading for my closet. I was borrowing trouble, worrying about a future that might never come to pass. The wee hours were the time when such demons of thought came to prey on vulnerable minds—it was the time I was most likely to worry about my teeth—and the best thing to do was to distract myself.

My closet, like my room, was a chamber of horrors from the late eighties and early nineties. There were clothes in there that had been too nice to get rid of, but looked too awful to wear, even when new. I dug through them, looking for something that might be salvageable.

At the back was a sand-washed red silk skirt, bought at an outlet store. It had potential. I took off my nightie and stepped into the skirt, and as I pulled it up past my butt I felt the crinkle and give of the rotten elastic in the waistband. The stretched-out skirt hung at the top of my hips, making me feel slender.

I looked at myself in the mirror inside the closet door, and grimaced. The skirt reached to that Queen Elizabeth

II length: the knee. It had reverse pleats that had permanently creased the fabric, and the fading would show if I took them out.

Garbage. Or scrap material, although I already had boxes of scraps that I never used.

I dug some more, and found an old pair of jeans. Calvin Klein.

I remembered these jeans. I'd loved them. I'd thought they made my butt look small, which was something Levi's never could do. I'd always envied those women whose thighs were so slim and free of saddlebags that Levi's flattered them, and on whom the jeans looked comfortable and loose instead of like dark blue sausage casing. It seemed that there were some who were born to look good in jeans, and some who were not.

I was not. I was a tailored wool sort of creature, dark colors preferable for their minimizing effect. No pockets to inflate my thighs, no pleats to pouch my tummy, no waistband to create a roll of flab above.

I pulled on the jeans, jumping up and down in my bare feet as I tried to get them up my hips. I looked in the mirror, at the gaping V of belly and panty that the open zipper revealed.

I hadn't grown any taller since I'd worn the jeans, but I'd certainly grown larger.

I remembered once when one of Mom's old friends had come to visit, and they'd sat looking at photos together. They'd laughed at how thin they'd once been, at how at the time they'd thought the opposite. Now it was my turn to do the same, and to wonder, as well, if ten years from now I'd think my twenty-nine-year-old self slender, and dream of once again being this size.

I took off the jeans and pulled my nightie back on, and sat on the flowered throw rug in the center of the room, looking at the ring with mosquito netting hanging above my bed, looking at the posters of Baroque cherub-filled art, looking at the inexpertly painted columns and arches on the wall beside my bed, put there in a juvenile effort to recreate a Victorian illustration I'd once seen for Sleeping Beauty.

Ten years had not brought me as far from my teenage self as I had thought it would. I lived on my own, but in some ways I was still in a fairy tale, waiting for Prince Charming, for my wedding with the white gown and the carriage and horses, the arch of flowers, and my suburban castle where my future little princesses and princes would romp in well-garbed splendor.

Deep in my heart, I believed that my life would not really begin until I found the right guy and got married. I didn't know why I believed that, or where the idea had come from, but there it sat. It was like I was a jockey at the starting gate, waiting for someone to show up with my horse.

Which was stupid, really. What was this I was doing in the meantime, if not living my life?

In ten years, I either wanted to have a family started, or I wanted to be financially secure, and possessed of the same ease and style of Ms. DeFrang, whose bedroom curtains, cushions and duvet I had sewn. One way or another, I didn't want to find myself at thirty-nine, sitting on my old bedroom floor, moaning about my weight gain and wondering when my life was going to get started.

Maybe I would never get married, never have children. Maybe my fate was to be an entrepreneur, and have employees and my own private sweat shop, or maybe I would give up self-employment and end up in management at a clothing manufacturer. Maybe I'd eventually have my *own* company, heading it like Gert Boyle headed Columbia Sportswear.

I was not going to let myself become a groundhog. Even if I had to live at home for the next five years, I would not let that happen. I would keep working, I would keep dating. I would keep living.

Mom would die, eventually. Dad would die, eventually. I would be alone, eventually. It was like I'd told the teen beauty queen, Bethany: it was my life, to make what I would of it, for I was the one who would be left to live it. It might as well be a life that I liked.

The future might hold horrid things, but I resolved that one of them was not going to be Hannah O'Dowd, wondering where her life had gone.

"Dad. I thought you'd be gone already," I said, coming into the kitchen. It was nearly 9:00 a.m., and Dad was sitting at the table, an empty cereal bowl with bits of bran flakes stuck to the sides sitting beside the paper. A banana peel hung over the edge of the counter.

"She won't be ready to go until eleven."

"I know," I said. I got a bowl out of the cupboard and a box of Rice Krispies. "We've got everything ready, don't we?"

The living room had been completely rearranged, a bed put in there for Mom. She wasn't strong or stable enough yet to safely climb and descend the stairs to her own bedroom, and Dad could not carry her. The bed in the living room had seemed the best solution, although I knew Mom would hate it, and not just because the bedspread didn't match the couch.

We'd also altered the toilet in the bathroom, attaching rails that made the fixture look like a white porcelain armchair. One of Dad's friends had built a temporary ramp for the front steps. We'd rented a collapsible wheelchair, and Mom had chosen a walker with four wheels and hand brakes that she would use until she was steady enough for a cane.

I hated these alien, physical presences in the house, with their stench of disability and illness. It was as though our house had been contaminated with hospital DNA, and started to grow medical features.

But at the same time that I hated the aluminum tubing, the gray rubber wheels and the plywood ramp, I was grateful that they existed, and intrigued enough by their strangeness that I had taken a spin around the living room in the wheelchair—and discovered in the process that end tables and stools needed to go into storage to keep the pathways clear.

"I think we're set," Dad said. "I can take care of anything else as it comes up."

I poured milk on my cereal, listening to it crackle and pop just as the box promised, and carried it carefully to the table, the milk threatening to slosh over the rim.

"And the nurse will come this afternoon?" I asked.

"Yes."

We were silent, as I started eating and Dad stared at the paper. My cereal had reached that pleasantly half-soggy, half-crunchy stage when he spoke again.

"Hannah?"

"Mmm?"

"Your mother and I were talking last night."

I nodded. "Yeah?"

"We think you should go back to Portland."

I stared at him, masticated Krispies pushed into my cheek. "What? Why?"

"It wasn't my idea, it was hers. But the more I thought about it, I saw she was right. There's no reason for you to stay down here and take care of her."

"But—"

"I can do it," he said.

My disbelief must have shown.

"The nurse will be here to help, and your mother may have been slowed down, but she can still tell me what to do. There's no reason for you to give up your life in Portland to come down here. She doesn't want that."

"And I don't want to abandon her!" I didn't want to abandon her to a house full of old banana peels and Dad, rough and awkward, helping her bathe. I didn't want to abandon her to whatever excuse for food he would come up with, or to lying in the living room ignored while he turned on the TV and let it blare.

"You're not abandoning her. If I wasn't here she'd need you, but I *am* here. It's my job to take care of her. I'm her husband. The last thing she wants—that either of us wants—is to be a burden to you."

How could I say I didn't trust him to have the competence to care for his wife? That I would rather be burdened than fear that Mom was being kept in a home-style nightmare of a care center?

There was no way to say it. And even as I rebelled against being kicked out of the house, a small guilty part of me was relieved that this was not going to be my burden. Not yet, at least.

"I can come down once or twice a week, though, can't I?" I asked.

"Of course you can. We didn't mean you shouldn't visit. We just don't want you to stay."

"Thanks. I guess," I said.

"If it makes you feel any better, you can do the grocery shopping when you come down. And the laundry. And someone is going to have to take care of the yard."

"Okay, okay!"

"You're a good girl, Hannah. Don't worry about us. We're going to be all right."

Twenty-Four

Green Piqué

"How's your mom doing?" Robert asked.

"Better, bit by bit," I said. I was at Butler & Sons, in Pioneer Place Two, dropping off a load of pants. It had been two weeks since Dad and Mom had sent me back to Portland. I'd visited them several times, and was slowly growing less surprised to find Mom still breathing and the house free of filth, fires and giant mayonnaise jars.

"That's gotta be rough," Robert said.

I shrugged. "I'm almost getting used to it. Isn't that peculiar?"

"I suppose you have to, after a time," he said, sounding uncertain.

"I suppose."

Day to day I *had* gotten used to it, but at unguarded moments fears for Mom would rise again to the surface and threaten to drown me. It was as if there was a huge subconscious reservoir of grief, waiting for its opportunity to burst forth in a messy emotional geyser.

And what was worse, anything sad or emotional to do with mothers or death could make me weepy-eyed now, whereas before I'd been left dry and sneering. Songs, movies, greeting cards, you name it, I'd weep at it. At least I hadn't descended to the depths of weeping at television commercials. Yet.

"I'm off in fifteen minutes, for lunch," Robert said. "You want to join me? Just, you know...as friends."

I remembered the last time I had refused, and he'd caught me reading the paper in the atrium when I'd said I had to run. I couldn't be such a witch's tit and refuse him again, especially when he'd been so thoughtful about Mom each time I came in.

"Sure, why not? I'll go window-shop until you're ready."

"Great!"

So I went and sniffed body lotions at Victoria's Secret, and pawed through the clearance rack seeking that one miraculous five-dollar nightie that wouldn't make me look droopy-breasted or lumpy-butted. The floor under the circular rack was littered with the crumpled bodies of fallen lingerie, as if the teddies and gowns had leaped from their hangers, committing suicide to end forever the indignity of being considered has-beens.

I wanted to save a lavender silk-satin set of boxer pajamas from whatever horror next awaited—an outlet store? a bargain bin, where its labels would be torn out, its identity erased?—but alas, my watch said Robert was waiting.

He was standing by the fountain in the center of the atrium when I emerged from the corridor. "Fishing for lunch money?" I asked.

"Or meter money. Don't think none of us hasn't done it, getting here before the place opens."

"You park on the street?" I asked, making conversation as we headed for the subterranean food court.

"No, I usually take the bus. I live just south of town, on Barbur. It's cheaper to leave the car at home."

At least he had a car, that was something.

He smelled of cologne, and I felt a little odd walking next to him, outside the store, as if we really knew each other. He had a shuffling, lazy gait, and was tall—taller than Scott. Tall enough to make me feel short and small, and not in a good way. If I ever hugged him, my cheek would rest against one of his spongey pecs.

"I'll meet you back here," I said, when we reached the court. It was late enough that the worst of the lunch crowd had scurried back to their cubicles, and most of the tables were free.

"No, hey, I asked you to lunch, let me get it."

I waved him off, and moved away. "Nah, don't worry about it," I said. I wanted to avoid any sense of obligation.

"I get a discount—" he called after me.

I pretended to not hear, and hurried 'round the circle of vendors, not wanting to look back and see him forlorn, backlit by a pizza display case.

Although pizza would have been nice. I settled instead on a turkey and provolone sandwich from a deli, feeling healthy and pure for doing so. Chinese food would have been good, but then I'd be burping up that taste the rest of the afternoon, and worried that my clients would smell it on my breath.

We met again at a table at the raised section in the center of the eating area, beside a rail that looked down on a tiled pool of water.

I liked the atmosphere of this food court more than

that of most restaurants. The ceiling was covered with plastic panels that resembled clouds, and behind them was darkness studded with tiny glowing stars, leaving the room just dim enough to be soothing. Water poured from lion heads in several fountains, lit from beneath to a turquoise glow, the gurgling water disguising the noise of voices.

"Your salad looks good," I said, sitting and arranging my tray of food.

"I've got to lose some weight. I must have gained thirty pounds since I went back to school."

"You're in school?" I asked, surprised. Preconceived notions were teetering, ready to plunk into the fountain.

"I'm getting my teaching degree. You think I want to be wearing golf shirts the rest of my life?" he asked, smiling, and plucking at the forest green piqué he wore.

"Huh. I didn't know."

"I've just got one course to finish up over the summer. I've done my student teaching, and should find out in the next week or two if I've gotten one of the jobs I applied for."

"Teaching what?"

"High school history, plus some coaching."

I looked at him, my perspective changing. Teaching high school might not be the most lucrative goal, but it was a highly respectable one. Of course, he probably had piles of student loans it would take an eternity to pay off.

"Are you going to P.S.U.?" I asked, thinking of Cassie, and Jack the Musician and Student.

"Uh-huh."

"My housemate is dating a guy who's in the teaching

program there. I'm not sure how far along he is. Jack Fogarty—do you know him?''

''Yeah, I've met him once or twice. Small world, huh? But I didn't know you lived with Cynthia!''

''Cynthia?''

''Isn't she your housemate? Jack's her boyfriend, isn't he? Or do I have the wrong guy in my head?''

''Long hair, works at a pub?'' I asked.

He made a moue of his lips, as we stared at each other in silence. ''Uh-oh,'' he said.

''Yeah, uh-oh.''

I'd seen Jack late last night, at our house, heading from Cassie's room to the bathroom, dressed only in saggy white briefs. ''You sure he didn't break up with Cynthia a couple months ago?''

''I don't think so.''

''Ah, crap,'' I said. ''Excuse the language. Who is Cynthia?''

''She's in the teaching program, she entered the same time I did. She came straight from undergrad, she can't be more than twenty-three. I don't know her well, but enough for chatting, and of course when she started dating Jack everyone knew, since he was in the program, too.''

''How does he even have *time?*'' I asked plaintively, not expecting an answer. ''God! What is wrong with men?''

Robert held up his hands. ''Hey, I don't know what's up with him.''

''Oh, I didn't mean you. You seem like a nice guy. But my housemate is going to be crushed. Dammit! Why did he have to be such a jerk? She liked him!''

''You're going to tell her?''

"Well of course I'm going to tell her."

"You know what they say about the messenger," Robert warned.

"If it were me, I'd want to know."

"Would you, really?"

"Of course. Oh, crap. This happened to her once before. Her ex cheated on her. She is *not* going to take this well." I glared at Robert, but it wasn't him I was thinking about.

I was thinking of Jack. Jack with his face like Keanu Reeves, with his acoustic guitar, with his lanky build and long hair. Jack, smiling with those white, slightly crooked teeth, pretending to not be the dog that he was.

A thought that was an insult to the canine species, who showed far more fidelity than one Jack Fogarty.

"Maybe it's not what it seems…" Robert said, trailing off as he heard his own words.

"Yeah, right. What an asshole. How could he do that?"

Robert shrugged a shoulder. "It's not *such* a big deal. It happens, you know."

I narrowed my eyes. "'It happens'?"

"It's not like he was engaged to either of them."

"That makes it okay?"

"No, not okay, but it's not like he broke a vow. It happens. He probably just couldn't decide between them."

My second impression of Robert, as kindly future teacher, shattered and tinkled away. "You see nothing wrong with that?"

"Maybe he should have made it a little clearer that he wasn't being exclusive with your friend. He probably didn't think it was that big a deal. It happens. He's just a guy, trying to figure things out.''

Was this the male version of nonjudgmental compassion? Did he think he was being fair and kind? Or *reasonable?*

I'd suddenly lost my appetite for Robert's company. I unfolded a couple of my oversupply of napkins and wrapped up my turkey sandwich—it had cost six-fifty, after all—and stood.

"Where are you going?" Robert asked, voice high-pitched in surprise. "You're leaving?"

"Yes," I said, gathering up my purse.

"Why?"

I looked at him, with his puffy-faced doofus expression. "It happens," I said.

I ate the rest of my sandwich in my car, spilling bits of lettuce and turkey down my shirt and into the spaces around the driver's seat, worrying about how upset Cassie was going to be, and fussing mentally over all those Dear Abby columns I'd read over the years, where no firm conclusion was ever drawn as to whether or not a friend should tell that a mate is cheating.

My instinct was to tell her. Warring with it was the wish to not hurt her.

Maybe I could tell Jack I knew, and let him do the right thing. It was a possibility, but at some point I know I'd blow it. Cassie would tell me it was over with Jack, and then two or three weeks or months down the road a comment would accidentally slip out that proved I'd known about the cheating before she had, and then what would she feel? Betrayed by me. Friendless.

And friends were those who stayed by you, when the men were jerks.

I could lie well enough in the present. It was the future that I couldn't handle.

I needed to talk it over with someone before I made a move based on emotion alone. I was furious with Jack, more furious than I would have been with a guy who had done the same to me.

When you're involved with someone, you put up with all sorts of garbage in hopes of continuing the relationship.

When it's your friend who's been wronged, there's nothing to mitigate the hate for the guy you never thought was good enough for her to begin with. You want to exterminate him.

At three o'clock I drove to Joanne's, for our appointment. She'd had three husbands and therefore seemed a good person to ask what to do. When I got there, though, she was on the phone, and the phone rang every time she hung up. She barely managed to tell me what I needed to do with the armload of garments she gave me. No help there.

My next appointment was with a retired judge who greeted me at the door in his bathrobe and slippers, white curls of chest hair showing between his ratty terry-cloth lapels. His wife had hired me to alter his pants, which kept sliding off his nonexistent butt. He was a short and wiry guy, bald and liver-spotted, hunched forward, and with that gleam in the eye that told you he was more goat than man.

Or were goats and men one and the same?

"You're a hot little number, aren't you?" he said by way of hello.

Somehow I restrained myself from kneeing him in the groin and dropping an elbow on the back of his neck. "A real firecracker," I said, without smiling.

He cackled, and the gleam in his eye started looking more like a twinkle. "So you're a toughie. I've seen the likes of you," he said, and made a couple boxing feints.

I tried to keep from laughing. "I carry sharp scissors, and am going to be fitting your pants," I said, with a meaningful look meant to imply all that could befall his privates if he were not careful. "Behave yourself."

He cackled again and let me in.

"You're not single, are you?" he asked ten minutes later while I was pinning the waistband of his slacks. "Don't tell me a beautiful girl like you is single."

"Afraid so."

"What, you chase them off with those scissors?"

I snorted.

"You like men, don't you?" he asked.

"When they behave."

"Ha! Might as well be a lesbian, then."

I squinted up at him. He was not what I would ever have imagined a retired judge to be.

"There's a lesbian going to come visit in half an hour. She's a friend of my wife's. I keep suggesting a threesome, but she just laughs."

"Can't imagine why," I said, checking the hang of the pants, dismally aware that he wasn't wearing underpants. He didn't have a hard-on, but I could see he preferred to hang on the right.

"I'll tell you something, that you might find useful."

"Hmm?" I said, down on my knees pinning the cuffs.

"You know, if you're on a date and a guy starts getting fresh. If he starts wanting more from you that you want to give out. Hell, use it even if he starts something, and his moves are bad and you change your mind.''

''Use what?'' I asked, getting curious.

''Tell him he has bad breath. Guaranteed, he'll go flatter than a blown tire.''

I laughed. ''I'll have to remember that one.''

''Girl used that on me once, in the back seat of a Chevy. Never could get it up again with her.''

''Can I ask you for a bit of advice?'' I asked, sitting back on my heels. The man used to be a judge, he should have a good answer. He had to have seen this type of situation a thousand times, if he hadn't been involved in it himself.

''Shoot.''

I briefly outlined the Cassie situation. ''How should I handle it?''

''You're in a lose-lose situation,'' he said. ''Sorry.''

''That's it?''

He shrugged.

''Well, what do you think of this Jack guy, and what he did?'' I asked.

''Men take what they can get.''

''What does that mean?''

He shrugged again. ''It happens.''

I was tempted to take out my scissors.

I got home at dusk, no wiser on what to do. I could ask Louise—her being a trained counselor and all—but it didn't feel right to share such a secret with her before sharing it with Cassie.

The house was quiet when I let myself in, Cassie already at work at the pub. I ran upstairs with my pile of garments and hung them up, then came back down to the dim living room, switching on lamps and the computer. The light on the answering machine was blinking, and I went and pressed the play button.

"Hannah? Pete, here. Where've you been? Give me a call, I'm off on Thursday."

Yeah, right, I'm going to call a guy who sneaks in without protection. Jerk. It had been a month and a half since our forest date, and this was the only time he'd called, that I knew about. Maybe he hadn't noticed I wasn't around. The ADHD and all.

More likely, he'd been sticking his cowled weenie into an un-booby-trapped woman.

I would have to go shoot Voodoo Pete a few times, to erase the annoyance of his call. His doll had a penis for a head, and a head for a penis. I had thought it apt.

The next message was for Cassie, from Jack, telling her he wouldn't be at work tonight as he wasn't feeling well.

Uh-huh. Maybe it was Cynthia's turn for a bit of Jack-in-the-pants luvin'.

The last message was from Scott.

"Hannah. How are you? How's your mom doing? I was just calling to check in. Give me a call if you feel like it."

Aw. Sweetie pie. Before giving myself a chance to think better of it I picked up the phone and dialed his home number.

"Hello?"

"Hi. It's Hannah."

"Hannah! Hi! How are you? How's your mom?" His voice was warm and deep, and I took the phone over to the futon and snuggled into a pillowed corner.

"I'm okay. Mom's doing okay, too, and Dad hasn't done her any serious damage, as far as I can tell. They'll

probably be suffering from malnutrition in another couple of months, but maybe Mom can teach Dad how to
cook by then.''

"Are you going down there this weekend?"

"Early Sunday, probably. I want to work in the flower
beds, so Mom doesn't have to worry about her roses.
I'll probably cook dinner, too. Maybe make a run to the
grocery store.''

"Would you like help?" he asked.

"Huh?"

"Help. You know. Help pulling weeds, mowing the
lawn, et cetera. I don't have anything planned for Sunday.''

"You don't have to do that," I protested.

"I know I don't *have* to. I want to. I've liked your
parents, the few times I've met them. You don't think
they'd mind, do you, if I helped? I mean, would it be
awkward?''

I gave a gurgling laugh. "Awkward? Only for me!
Dad has spent his entire life trying to get someone else
to mow the lawn for him. He'd probably try to make
you chop wood or wash his car, maybe reshingle the
roof. He wouldn't care why you're there, only that you
were free labor.''

"Then why awkward?" he asked.

"Mom will think you're my boyfriend. Or she'll think
you should be. I wouldn't hear the end of what a nice
boy Scott is.''

"Nothing wrong with that.''

"That would amuse you, wouldn't it?" I said. "I
wonder what your lawyer friend would think.''

"Oh. Well. I'm not seeing her anymore.''

"What?"

"We broke up—if you could call it that—a week and a half ago."

"Why?" I asked. And I wondered if his being at loose ends had anything to do with the desire to come spend Sunday with me and my parents.

That wasn't a fair thought, though. Throughout these past weeks Scott, even more than Louise and Cassie, had been attentive, always checking in and offering his assistance, asking if there was anything I needed done, or if I just wanted company.

I assumed he was more forward in his offers of company or help than Louise or Cassie because, having been there himself, he was not so afraid of not knowing what to say. His dad dying had been a hundred times worse than Mom's stroke, but still I felt there was an understanding between us that I didn't have with my other friends.

"She said my heart wasn't in it," Scott said. "She said she didn't have the time to waste, waiting for me to figure out how I felt about her."

"Ow."

"Not really. She was right, my heart wasn't in it, and it was relief I felt more than anything else when she ended it. I could never relax around her."

"So are you going back to the Internet?" I asked, hoping he'd say no. Not that I had any reason to have such a wish. Or was I becoming just a little possessive of Scott's time and attention?

I'd better watch myself. If I weren't careful, I could thoroughly screw up our comfortable foursome of friends.

"I don't think so. Not for a while, anyway. Summer's here. There are better things to do with my time."

"Like pull weeds at someone else's house?"

"Hey, you don't want my help, you don't have to take it," he said, and I couldn't quite tell if he was offended or joking.

"I just feel a little strange about it. You've been so thoughtful, I don't like to continue to impose."

"Oh, for God's sake. Hannah, you are so busy being independent all the time and taking matters into your own hands, you forget to let people help you."

"I don't want to be dependent on anyone," I said.

"It's not dependency! It's strength, to let someone help you."

"I don't see it," I grumbled.

"It's... Hell, I don't know how to explain it. I only understood it myself recently."

"I thought guys didn't like being helped. I thought they found it bossy."

"Yes! That's exactly it! And why don't guys like being helped? Because they think it means you think they aren't strong or smart enough to do it on their own. But when you're truly strong, you can admit ignorance or errors without it being a threat. You can admit you need help with something."

"Have you been talking to Louise? This sounds like something she would say," I said. It wasn't Scott's habit to ponder the workings of the mind and emotions, unless prodded to by one of us.

"Uh, maybe."

"What were you two talking about? Was she chastising you for something?" I was curious what could have driven him to such a conversation.

"Er. It's not important."

"Now I'm curious."

"Never mind! The pillows look nice on the couch. Did I tell you that?"

"Changing the subject?" I asked.

Had they been talking about me? It was paranoid to think so. And what would there have been to discuss, anyway?

"Yes, I'm changing the subject."

"Fine," I said. A little silence stretched between us, and I heard him shift positions. I wondered if he was sprawled on his leather couch, and was almost tempted to ask what he was wearing. I giggled. We could have phone sex.

"What?"

"Nothing." As if I could admit such a thing had crossed my mind!

I thought then about Cassie and Jack, and somehow it felt all right to tell Scott, in a way it wasn't all right to tell Louise. "I have a bit of a problem I could use some perspective on. Do you want to hear it?"

Of course he did. I outlined the situation to him.

"Asshole!" he said when I had finished.

"That's what I thought," I said.

"The guy has no sense of honor. Fucking asshole!"

"You know, you're the first guy I've talked to who thought so. The rest all said, 'It happens,' like it was no big deal."

"They have no honor. I would never do that. Shit! What a jerk! She's better off without him, you know."

"I know, but how do I tell her?" I asked.

"Christ. I can't believe someone would do that to Cass."

I let him rant a little longer, strangely comforted by

Lisa Cach

his response. Despite the profanity, it was chivalrous in comparison to what I'd heard from Robert and the goat-judge. *They* hadn't mentioned honor. *They* hadn't acknowledged that even in the twenty-first century there were standards of conduct to which a man should adhere.

Honor. I liked the sounds of that. It was the first time I had heard the word coming from the lips of a man in real life.

It was surprisingly touching.

"You're going to have to tell her, you know," he said. "I wouldn't trust him to break up with her on his own."

I sighed. "I know."

A few moments passed, and then, "So, am I coming with you on Sunday?"

"Let me think about it," I hedged.

"You're impossible."

"That's why you adore me."

He made a noise of disgust. "Good night, Hannah."

"Good night." I hung up, and smiled at the phone.

Twenty-Five

Percale Sheets

It was past midnight, and I was up sewing, waiting for Cassie to come home. I'd had a couple cups of instant cappuccino, which had only encouraged my mind to fret and fidget, thoughts leaping neurons in a frantic jig that was almost as unpleasant as the squishy, sour state of my stomach.

My half-finished wedding dress hung on the rack with the other clothes waiting to be altered. There was the usual backlog of men's pants, in shades of brown, green and gray that belonged on a mouldy forest floor; Bethany's evening gown, which after much embarrassed pouting on the beauty queen's part it had been decided needed bigger falsies and a tighter built-in corset; two mother-of-the-bride dresses needing shortening; three wool women's business jackets to be taken in; and a mish-mash of skirts and dresses needing darts put in or taken out, hems adjusted, necklines changed, bodices shortened, et cetera, et cetera, et cetera.

It was no wonder I was working on another wrestling costume instead.

Elroy had paid me up front this time—no more

pseudo-psychic sessions in payment, thank you not so much! And a good thing, as I couldn't imagine his meager career continuing much longer after he wore this costume into the ring.

The bulldog costume had proved less than exciting to the wrestling audience, and the fur pants had lacked stretch and were too hot. I'd warned him of both those facts before making them, but he'd paid as much attention to my advice then as he had to the advice I'd given him yesterday, on this new costume: you're going to look ridiculous.

He wanted to be Sasquatch. The man was strong, but short. Who ever heard of a five-six Sasquatch?

And what was worse even than the height issue, he was having me make him a hairy, domed cap that would give him the supposed sloping, pointed cranium of a Big Foot.

Maybe he could hire himself out to kid's parties.

The pants were all right this time, though. They were a stretchy lycra knit, and I was attaching long tufts of brown wool to them with a glue gun. Elroy would have had to have been CEO of a psychic line to afford to pay me to sew the stuff on by hand.

Short hairy legs, bare chest, pointed head. He either had nerve, or pink pudding for brains.

I listened to the radio, attached hair, and strained my ears for the sound of Cassie's car. It was past 1:00 a.m. when I finally heard it, and set down my glue gun.

"Hey, workaholic," she said a couple minutes later, poking her head into my sewing room.

"Hey, tavern wench."

"I'm beat. And I reek. I'm going to take a shower and go to bed. You okay?"

"Yeah. Why wouldn't I be?"

"Just checking," she said, and headed toward her room.

I got up and followed her, and stood in her doorway as she unbuttoned her white shirt. "I met someone today who knows Jack," I said. I might as well get it over with.

"Oh? A friend?" she asked, pausing in her undressing. She was smiling, the way one smiles when there is a surprise chance to talk about the guy you like.

"Classmate, at P.S.U."

"What'd he say about him?"

She was expecting something nice, or at the worst something harmless along the lines of, "He doesn't know him well, but says he seems like an okay guy."

"He says Jack is dating one of the other students, a girl named Cynthia," I said, and grimaced as if doing so would keep the words from hurting her.

"What?" she said, her face going blank at the shock. And then she relaxed, and smiled. "Cynthia? Oh, he's misinterpreting. They had to do a project together, is all. They're just friends. I know all about her."

"Really?" All that angst had been for nothing? "Thank God. He seemed so sure that Jack was Cynthia's boyfriend—he said everyone in the program knew they were seeing each other," I babbled, relieved. All that worry! All that fuss! Over nothing! "I should have known it was just gossip. A man and woman can never be friends without people speculating."

"He said everyone knew?" she said slowly, sounding uncertain now.

"He was probably exaggerating. Hey, I didn't mean to make you doubt Jack, if there's no reason," I said, backpedaling.

She picked up the phone by the bed.

"You're not going to call him, are you?" I squeaked, suddenly seeing myself in the center of a messy emotional scene, getting blamed for all the trouble. Jack would hate me.

"He called in sick, he'd better be at home," she said, dialing. She waited as the connection was made, and as the phone rang. And rang. And finally was answered. I could only hear Cassie's side of the conversation.

"Russ? It's Cassie. Can I talk to Jack? ...Could you wake him up for me?

I don't care, this is really important. It's an emergency."

Accusingly, "He's not home, is he? Russ, come on. Don't lie for him. I know he's not home. I know about Cynthia."

A long silence on Cassie's end. She wasn't facing me, but I could see her head tilting forward, her shoulders hunching in, a quiver starting across her back as she listened to whatever Russ, Jack's roommate, was saying.

"No, don't leave a message. Thanks for leveling with me."

"Yeah, well, thanks. 'Bye."

She turned around and there were tears in her eyes. She blinked, and they spilled down her cheeks.

"The snake," she said softly.

I came toward her, then stopped as she suddenly shrieked, grabbed the covers to her bed, and ripped them off. She tore at the sheets until they, too, came loose, and threw them on the floor, the mattress pad following.

"Cunt-licking liar! Sheep fucker!"

Sheep fucker?

"Ass-tonguing pecker head!" She scooped up the bedding and I backed out of the way as she went to the door and tossed it into the hallway, another screech ripping from her throat.

"Cass?" I asked softly, scared. I'd never seen her like this. Not serene Cassie, for whom every event had a purpose and harmony was the key to life.

"I have to bleach the sheets," she said, her voice cold. She stood motionless, staring at the pile of linens in the hall, her arms hanging by her sides. "I can't sleep in them until I wash out his smell."

She turned and looked at me, and the corners of her mouth twisted down, her head tilting to the side, her beautiful green eyes full of pain. "Why does this keep happening to me?"

I shook my head. "I don't know." I almost said that it wasn't her fault, men were jerks, Jack was an asshole, she deserved better—but none of it would answer the question. None of it could explain why she had to be hurt again.

"Was I not smart enough for him? Or too poorly educated? I almost got my B.A., I was just a few credits short, but maybe that doesn't compare to someone getting a master's." She looked at me for confirmation.

I didn't know what to say.

"I mean, it doesn't make me a loser, that I didn't finish, does it?"

"You're a hundred times wiser than he is. You're not the one who hurts people," I said.

"Am I too old? Maybe my butt sags too much. She's younger than he is—she's probably got perky breasts."

"I don't think it's about you," I said. "It's him. He's messed up. He has to be, to do this to both you and that Cynthia. There's nothing wrong with you."

"Then why wasn't I good enough?" she asked, plaintive. And then the tears came.

I closed the distance between us and held her.

Cassie came up the basement stairs and into the kitchen, the sound of the dryer rumbling softly behind her. It was 3:00 a.m., and we had polished off the ice cream in the freezer and moved on to the bottle of red wine a client had given me at Christmas.

Cassie rejoined me at the small nook table in the corner of the kitchen, both of us in our bathrobes now, but unwilling to give up the night. Without Jack to confront, there was no resolution for her, only a wounded heart.

"Do I get a Voodoo Jack doll?" she asked, pulling her feet up onto the chair, her knees reaching nearly to her chin. Her hair was still wet from her shower, her pale face touched with color only where the wine had stained her lips.

"Of course. What do you think, give him two faces?"

"And two dicks, neither of which will stay in his pants," she said. "Everyone thinks he's such a nice guy."

"I might not have liked the age difference between you, but I thought he was a decent guy. I would never have guessed he would do such a thing."

"No one would have. I'm not a vengeful person, but I feel like everyone should know what he did. I almost feel like everyone *has* to know, for Jack's own good," she said.

"That is an interesting way to look at it. Public humiliation for *his* good."

"No, really," Cassie said, perking up. "In some part of himself, he knows that what he did is wrong. He has to be ashamed, deep down. It's like a murderer who wants to confess and be punished. He's not going to be able to live with himself until he gives penance."

"And you're the one to force him to it? It sounds more like revenge than maintaining the natural order, O Mother Goddess."

"He has to be expecting this to come," she said. "He must know it couldn't go on forever."

"I think you're giving him more credit than he deserves," I said. "He never struck me as being particularly perceptive or introspective."

"Yes, and that's why he needs to be shunned. He might not have the courage to face his own guilt, so others need to help him. It's tho only way hc'll become a better person. It will help him to grow."

"That is an interesting theory," I said carefully, a little unnerved by the intensity of her expression. Cassie was the only person I knew who could possibly turn vengeance into a growth experience for the victim. She was either unwilling to admit her own desire to take a Garden Weasel to Jack's privates, or she was truly more evolved than I could ever hope to be.

"I'll tell everyone at the pub what he did—coworkers, supervisors, customers. You tell that clerk at the clothing store to tell everyone in the teaching program. Everyone has to know.''

''Won't that be humiliating, for you?''

She blinked in surprise. ''Why? I did nothing wrong.''

I shrugged. We sipped wine, and listened to the tossing of the dryer in the basement. I yawned, and thought about going to bed, but then Cassie spoke again.

''I thought I'd be able to tell by now, you know?'' She sounded depressed again, the fire of retribution dampened. ''I thought I had enough experience, I would know a jerk when I met one. Have I learned nothing?''

''Have any of us learned? Look at Louise, with that Derek. Look at me, still single despite my one-in-a-million campaign.''

Cassie made a derisive sound.

''What?''

''You, still single. Only because you want to be. You know your Mr. Right is sitting right in front of you.''

''Who?''

''Oh, come on, Hannah. Scott! Who else!''

I felt my cheeks heat, and perspiration break out under my arms. ''We're just friends. Like all of us are.''

''Not like all of us. He's half in love with you, and you'd see it if you wanted to look.''

''No he's not. He was dating that lawyer chick just a few weeks ago. He's not interested in me that way.'' I was protesting too much, and I suspected she knew it.

''I'm not going to try to convince you. It's what I meant a few months ago, when I told you it would happen when you were ready. He's been interested in you since you moved up here, but he's not going to risk anything until he's sure you're open to it.''

"But he belongs to Louise,'' I said.

"That was ten years ago. It's ancient history. The only reason he hangs out with us as much as he does is to be near you.''

"I didn't realize... Scott, and me?''

"Have you never thought about it? Honestly?''

I didn't want to admit that I had. Whatever little flames of interest were in my heart, they were fragile and might blow out in the breath of conversation. I was going to feel weird enough in the same room with both Cassie and Scott now, without her knowing I might have more than a strictly friendly interest in him.

"I'm sorry,'' Cassie said, before I could think of anything suitable to say. "It's the wine, and it's been a bad night. I didn't mean to say any of that.''

"There's nothing to apologize for,'' I said.

She ran a finger over the rim of her glass, then pushed it away from her and shrugged. "Whatever was going to happen between you two, I've screwed it up by talking about it. Now you'll be standoffish to Scott, afraid to act natural. I've blocked your chakra,'' she said, smiling.

"I don't know why you'd be eager to have us paired off.''

"I want to see someone in a good relationship.''

"It wouldn't be upsetting, after this thing with Jack?'' I asked. "Since when do the broken-hearted like to see others in love?''

The last traces of angry, disturbed Cassie, the Cassie of ripping bedsheets and vengeful schemes, faded away, and her features softened into the peaceful, all-knowing expression I was used to.

"Hannah, don't you understand?" she said. "The happiness of my friends is my own happiness."

Jack had no idea of what he had lost.

Twenty-Six

Running Tights

"They always lie. Why do they always lie? It's not like we're not going to notice," Louise said, gesturing into the air.

We were hiking the Wildwood Trail, from the zoo parking lot through the Hoyt Arboretum all the way to Pittock Mansion, with its view over the north end of the city. It was a popular route, especially on a Saturday, with runners, dogs and chatting pairs passing us or being passed every few minutes.

"Did he think I wouldn't notice that his claim to an average weight did not correspond to the sixty extra pounds hanging off his belly?" she asked. "Although I certainly couldn't tell by that photo."

In an effort to cleanse her dating palate of the taste of Derek the Divorced and Uninterested, Louise had at last succumbed to the lure of Internet dating. The guy she'd chosen had looked cute in his picture—a picture, it turned out, he had chosen with a clever eye to self-flattery.

"It's like catalog shopping for clothes," I said. "You have to be suspicious if the model is sitting down or has her arms crossed over her waist. The outfit probably makes her look like a stump."

"And baseball caps. I'll bet ninety percent of the guys who put up photos wearing a baseball cap are bald."

"Can't blame them for trying," I said.

"He didn't wear the cap to the coffee shop, though, and every time he got embarrassed he rubbed his head. It was like he was polishing it. I was tempted to squirt a bit of Turtle Wax on for him, maybe hand him a chamois. And it wasn't just his looks he lied about."

"Oh?"

"He said he had a Ph.D. in psychology. Nope. Hasn't done his dissertation yet. He said he loved to travel, especially abroad. He's been to England—ooo! How foreign!—and the rest of his travel has been road trips in the U.S. He said he loved kayaking. He's only kayaked once, three years ago."

"None of those are exactly lies," I said, mostly to egg her on.

"And he had soft little hands, with pointy fingers."

"Eww. Baby mouse paws," I said.

"Can you imagine hands like that touching you?"

We contemplated such a horror in shared revulsion.

"He was nice, though, wasn't he?" I asked. "I mean, he wasn't what you were looking for, but he wasn't a jerk, or a looney tunes."

She gave an exaggerated sigh. "Too nice. That crap guys give about women not liking the nice guys, they don't get it. Nice doesn't mean being so passive and needy that you let women walk all over you. His ex tricked him into marriage with the old 'I'm pregnant and I'll abort it' routine. Can you believe that still works?"

"At least he tried to do what he thought was right."

"But what type of idiot doesn't know what he's getting himself into? Oh, yeah, like that marriage is going to work. Poor kid would be better off not being born, with a mom like that and an idiot father. Of course, his wife 'miscarried' shortly after the wedding."

"Whoever said men were bright about relationships?" I asked. "They're like bumpkins visiting a city for the first time. Some are sweet, some are rednecks, but not one has a clue."

"And then they can't believe it when things go bad," she said.

I liked it when Louise got into rant mode. There were times I thought she'd as soon stomp on a man as kiss one. Someday she'd be swept off her feet, and I hoped to be around to see it happen. It would be fodder for merciless teasing.

"The men I talk to on the crisis line, who are getting divorced," she went on, "all they do is cry and talk about killing themselves. Or maybe killing their wives, and then themselves. They can't handle it, they have no idea what's going on and they can't imagine a future without her." She stopped her rant for a moment as I stepped behind her, letting a jogger by.

"The women getting divorced, though, all they care about is ownership of the house."

"That makes women sound like the mercenaries, and men like the romantics."

"What makes a person romantic?" she asked. "Ideals crafted from fairy tales and one-dimensional beliefs about people and relationships? It doesn't scream of intelligence."

"But maybe we need a little of that type of magic in our lives. Reality is too cold and gray. I want to believe in the happily-ever-after, and a love that never dies."

"Despite experience?" she asked.

"Yes."

"What type of unrealistic philosophy is that?"

"If you go into dating with a bitter attitude, you're not going to attract a warm-hearted guy," I said. "It's like there's some sort of karmic dating force out there, giving back what you put out."

"Put out?" she snickered.

"I didn't mean that in a sexual way," I said, chiding.

"I don't see how this karmic dating has benefited you so far. Look at that Pete creep."

"But I got what I asked for, didn't I? All I was interested in was his body, and that's all he gave me. Or I hope that's all he gave me. I haven't had a pelvic exam yet."

A male jogger approached us, and I stepped behind Louise again. He was a good-looking guy, early thirties, dark hair and a model's jaw. He also seemed to be lacking a jock-strap under his running tights.

He nodded to us and passed by.

"Did you see that?" I asked.

"How could I not?"

"Do you think he knows it's sticking out? It's like he's got a tree branch growing out of his groin."

"He's got to know," Louise said. "Maybe he gets his kicks letting it flop around in public. Maybe he thinks it turns us on."

"Makes me think of a dog licking his penis where everyone can see it. Ugh."

"I thought you were the one obsessed with the male organ?"

"Only in the proper setting," I said. I turned and looked back down the trail, but the jogger was long gone. "Think he'll come back?"

"You wish."

We walked in silence for a short ways. The trail was cut into the side of a forested slope, and on our right we could look down through the trees and see glimpses of the Japanese Garden in Washington Park.

"That date has pretty much taken care of any desire I had to meet someone right now," Louise said.

"One date and you're finished?"

She shrugged.

"You really don't care about getting married, do you?" I asked. "Or even about getting involved." I knew we'd had this discussion before, but it was as though I had to keep checking that it could really be true.

"Not particularly. I feel like a freak for saying it, but I'm happy alone. I like having my apartment to myself. I like doing my own thing, and since I don't want to have children, there's no pressure to find someone soon."

"Don't you miss the sex?"

She shrugged, as if embarrassed to admit that she wasn't a steaming mass of frustrated hormones. "You know, I never could fall asleep with a guy in my bed. I think I'd rather spend winter with a down comforter than a man."

"You were happy enough with Scott while it lasted, weren't you?"

"That was a long time ago. There was the novelty factor that made it bearable."

"Was he lousy in bed?" I asked, and then felt my cheeks heat. I couldn't believe I'd asked that. We had known each other long enough that we felt free to inquire into the skills of men we were dating, but never had I asked about Scott's past performance. I wasn't sure I even wanted to know.

"He was attentive. Perceptive," Louise said. "A quick learner. I imagine he's learned a lot since we were together," she said, a leer in her voice. "Why do you want to know?"

"Just curious," I mumbled.

"He was one of those guys who likes to sleep with an arm draped over you, and he'd snore right in your ear. I couldn't sleep like that. Could you?"

"Probably. I like snuggling up to someone."

"Hey, what happened last weekend?" she asked suddenly. "Scott thought he was going to go down to Roseburg with you."

"I decided to go on Saturday, instead, and spend the night. It was too far to ask him to drive on his own, so I told him not to come."

The truth of the matter was that Cassie, as she'd predicted, had weirded me out about the whole Scott thing, and I couldn't see us spending that much time alone in a car together, and didn't want him doing yardwork at my parents' house as if they were potential in-laws he was trying to impress.

I didn't know *what* I was feeling about Scott. He was cute; we enjoyed each other's company; I had, admittedly, used my new vibrator and put his face on the fantasy man who was doing me; but still, I wasn't sure what it all added up to. I wasn't sure if it was worth enough to destroy the friendly ease we all shared, which would surely happen the moment Scott and I crossed the line from friendship to something more.

"I think he was disappointed," Louise said.

I played with the idea of asking her if she thought Scott had a thing for me, and if he did, if it bothered her.

I couldn't bring myself to do it. It was too embarrassing, and I didn't think she'd be able to give an honest answer. I mean, what could she say? She'd have to say it was fine, no matter what discomfort she felt, otherwise shc'd sound insanely possessive.

"He'll get over it," I said. Another cute jogger went by, nodding at us as he passed. We watched his rump flexing as he trotted away. "Do you suppose we could trip one, just to make him stop?"

"You're the horny one, you do it."

"Only if you'll help me drag him into the ferns so I can have my way with him," I said.

"No problem."

"You're a good friend."

"Don't I know it."

Twenty-Seven

Pale Gold Accessories

"You don't really want to go out with this guy," Cassie said. She was sitting on my bed while I tried on different sandals, checking which would go best with the soft pink floral sundress I'd made.

"Yes I do." I kicked off the brown ones, and tried the pair with the narrow pale gold straps. They were flats, so my legs looked shorter than I would have wished, but the brown sandals were just too heavy-looking.

She raised her brows, in a gesture that suggested I was fooling myself and that she knew what was really going on.

"What?" I asked.

"No, if you want to go out with him, you should."

A statement that immediately made me want to shake out of her whatever she was thinking. I don't know why I always asked for her advice, when I heeded almost none of it.

"Come on, what? Do you see it as doomed from the start?" I asked.

She looked at me, not answering.

"I think there's potential here. He seems to have everything in place," I said. I didn't sound very convincing.

"You go ahead and do what you have to."

"You're not half so harmless as you look," I told her. She smiled serenely.

Last week I'd realized that my birthday was fast approaching. Three more weeks, and I'd be thirty, and if I didn't do something quickly, I'd still be single. My plan to find a mate had sounded so simple and efficient four months ago, but somehow the time had slipped away, and I was no further along than I had been.

Unless I wanted to count Scott.

If I hadn't been attracted to him from the very beginning, though, maybe that meant there wasn't really any chemistry between us. Maybe it meant that whatever pull we might feel toward each other, it was there only because of familiarity and availability.

But if I'd first met him as a stranger, and not as Louise's ex-boyfriend, what would I have thought?

Oh, baby, come to Mama. That's what I would have thought.

Before I made any move in that direction, I had to be certain that Mr. One-in-a-Million was not waiting around the corner. I didn't want to miss out on my perfect match because I'd given up too soon and gotten together with a guy I'd known as a friend. I didn't want to settle.

So, I'd gone on a personal ad binge, both traditional newspaper and Internet. The *Oregonian, Willamette Week,* Yahoo!, AOL, Match.com, Matchmaker.com. Any personal ads out there, I'd sifted through them,

writing to any man within the desired age range who
had a college education, didn't smoke and didn't seem
to be an utter lunatic.

There were fewer of them than one might think. And
desperate creatures that they were, the same man was
often found on two or three sites.

Not that *I* was desperate for searching all the sites and
papers. Organized. Efficient. Practical. That's what I
was.

"How is your public humiliation project progress-
ing?" I asked, changing the subject from my dating wisdom or folly.

Cassie had confronted Jack the Two Timer the day
after her discovery of his perfidy. She had, she'd said,
been perfectly cordial in her ending of their liaison, and
had proceeded to detail the situation to every person
who crossed her path, whether they knew Jack or not.
She said it had proved therapeutic, and she had a new
understanding of talk therapy.

I wondered what Louise would have to say about such
a treatment plan.

"He's getting a paranoid look in his eyes," she said.
"He gets fidgety whenever someone looks at him, especially if they're talking to someone else at the time. I
have hopes that a nervous tic will soon develop."

"I'm surprised he can stand to still work there."

"I thought about hanging Voodoo Jack in the break
room, but Real Jack might steal him," she said. "Besides, I like shooting him."

That I knew. I'd finished Voodoo Jack only a few
days ago, but in that time I had heard the faint twang

of the rubber band gun and Cassie's version of his screams at all hours.

"I still wish I could have found a slingshot," I said. "Pellets would have thwacked so well."

"The rubber bands are good. At least I don't have to worry about cracking a window. I may burn him when I'm done, though. Would you mind?"

"Be my guest."

It was a short drive to the Irvington neighborhood, where I was to meet my date, Tyler, a thirty-eight-year-old computer engineer.

I had finally done it. The computer geeks were everywhere, and with few other options I had persuaded myself to meet one.

It seemed unfair, after all, to prejudge a man by his profession. Perhaps, as he claimed, he had artistic sensibilities, and read things other than tech magazines and science fiction. Perhaps he really did run marathons and practice Tai Chi—although I wasn't sure the Tai Chi was in his favor.

Maybe, just maybe, his sense of humor wasn't stuck in third grade, and maybe he wore an analog wristwatch, instead of some digital monstrosity with a built-in calculator and weather forecasts downloaded from a satellite.

And even if none of the above were true, he might have other redeeming qualities. Maybe he hadn't lied about an income that topped a hundred thousand a year, and his desire to start a family. Maybe his photo reflected reality.

One could hope.

I'd agreed to come to his house—perhaps not the wisest of choices, but he'd sent me a photo of it via e-mail, and I couldn't resist. It had been built in 1910, with three floors and over five thousand square feet. He was renovating it bit by bit, he'd written.

The Irvington neighborhood had a number of historic homes—"historic" being a relative term, in Portland—and I enjoyed my slow cruise down the tree-lined streets, looking at the big old houses and their gardens. It was late afternoon, the sun was still bright but with a hint of that warm golden tone that encouraged lazy strolling, as many were doing along the sidewalks.

I smelled freshly cut grass, and heard the ch-ch-ch of a sprinkler and the bouncing of a basketball in someone's driveway.

This was someplace I could see living.

The house was on a corner, huge and white and shaded by leafy trees. I parked next to the curb and walked up the brick path, taking in the yard that, while tended and neat, looked like nothing new had been planted for years.

I imagined myself taking on the role of gardener. Climbing roses for the trellises on the sides of the portico; lilacs in a hedge along the front, for privacy; the usual tulip bulbs for spring, and dahlias for summer. Mom would have some good suggestions, if I asked.

The paint on the house was sanded off in places, as if awaiting a fresh coat. Two of the small panes of glass in the sidelights were cracked. I was reminded of Dad's comments through the years about the pains of fixing up an old house, and couldn't help but be struck by the possibility—the synchronicity?—of ending up doing the same thing myself, with Tyler.

I rang the bell.

I caught a glimpse of movement through the side-lights, and then the door opened.

"Hannah? Hi."

"Hi." He was as cute as his photo: about five-eleven, a runner's build, blondish-brown hair a little too long, and a pleasant, if narrow, face. He was wearing an earring, though, a small sapphire stud. I hadn't seen that in the photo.

"Did you have any trouble finding the place?"

"It's kind of hard to miss," I said.

"Come in," he said, stepping back. "Careful, don't let Sassy out," he added, as an overweight marmalade cat brushed by his ankles. "She's an indoor cat. She's declawed—she wouldn't stand a chance out there."

I slunk inside. He'd told me in an e-mail that he had two cats, but somehow I'd manage to block the information from my consciousness. As long as he didn't start talking about "Kitty did this... Kitty did that..." maybe it would be okay.

Men with cats. It just wasn't right.

"Wow. Nice entryway," I said, and meant it. The floor was gleaming parquet, and opposite the front door was a curving staircase with a carved balustrade. There was no furniture, and nothing on the walls, but directly above us was a huge crystal chandelier that looked as if it had been stolen from Versailles.

"Thanks. It took me ages to decide on the floor, and you wouldn't believe how hard it is to find someone to do this kind of work. My friends kid me about how long

I take to make a decorating decision, but this is my dream house, you know? I want it to be perfect.''

"I don't blame you.''

"You want a tour?'' he asked.

"Yeah, sure. Do you want me to take off my shoes?'' He was barefoot, wearing khaki walking shorts and a clean white T-shirt. Given his own bare feet and his flawless floor, I didn't want to risk inflicting damage.

"No, that's all right. You're not wearing heels.''

I followed him from room to room, listening to his descriptions of what he had planned for each. Most of them were nearly empty, yet each had a single piece of furniture or a rug, or even just a box of stuff that told of what its future would be. The library had stacks of books on the floor. The formal living room had a marble fireplace and a gilt-framed mirror. The dining room had a massive sideboard. And so on, and under all of it there were the beautiful floors.

"And this is the ballroom,'' he said, leading me up the stairs to the top floor. "Or, the storage area. I keep all my junk up here, since it's going to be quite a while before I can get to this part of the house. I'm going to have to replace the roof in the next five years or so, anyway, and for all I know it could make a mess up here.''

"But what a lot of fun this room will be when it's finished,'' I said. The ceiling was low, and sloped on the sides because of the roofline, and looked more like a converted attic than a ballroom. "If I'd been a kid in a house like this, I would have loved roller skating up here.''

He laughed, but I wasn't sure he was amused. "Skates would be hell on the floors."

"Probably."

He led the way back downstairs. It was strange, but for all the empty space in the house, I was beginning to wonder if there was really any space in it for someone else. Tyler had plans for every room, and I wasn't getting the feeling he'd considered that his future wife might have her own ideas about the home they would share.

On the other hand, there was no reason for him to wait around for Ms. Right to show up, when there was a house to be renovated.

"Are you hungry?" he asked. "I can start dinner."

"I was kind of hoping we could take a little walk through the neighborhood first. It's such a pretty evening."

He grimaced. "I ran eight miles today. I'm kind of sore."

"Oh. Okay."

"No, we can go, just let's not make it a major hike or anything."

"Yeah, sure," I said.

I followed him to a back door off the kitchen, and wondered what the deal was. He was too tired for a walk? The only reason his running had seemed like a good thing to me was because it would mean he was in shape, and would have energy. It hadn't occurred to me that he might spend all that energy actually *running*.

What was the point of that?

I wondered if that was what all those gorgeous runners on the Wildwood Trail would be like, in person:

too tired to walk around the block. Probably too tired to have sex, too. "Come on, honey, go down on me. I'm too tired to do anything else." Like that was going to be a lot of fun for the woman, wearing out her jaw while he lay back and—

"Hannah? Is something wrong?"

"Huh? No, just daydreaming." I smiled at him as he put on his Teva sandals, then squinted at his toes. "Er... Is that nail polish you're wearing?"

He grinned, then slid his foot next to mine. "It matches your sandals. What a coincidence!"

"Do you always wear toenail polish?" I asked carefully. *What a coincidence,* indeed. If *this* was synchronicity, I wanted nothing of it.

"Only in the summer, and only gold."

"Why?" I asked, trying to not sound appalled.

"I like how it looks, so why not?"

Because you look like a Bohemian-wannabe fruitcake, that's why, I wanted to say. Toenail polish, good Lord. "Fair enough," I said instead.

"I'm not gay or anything. I'm just not going to be limited by other people's opinions. Does it bother you?"

"Hey, they're your toes. You can wear whatever you want on them."

Things improved during the walk. We talked about Portland, hiking in the gorge, movies we both liked or hated, and as we came back to the house we talked about work.

"You made that dress, really?" he asked, motioning me to a seat in the 1950's style, unrenovated kitchen.

"This? Piece of cake."

"Lemonade okay?"

"Great," I said, and he poured me a glass.

"How long did it take you to make it?"

"Two hours, give or take."

He stopped, pitcher of lemonade in hand. "You're kidding."

"No." I smiled uncertainly. "And it's my own pattern. Or, rather, I started with something from Butterick, then changed it to suit me."

"That's amazing. Really, Hannah, that's great. We are so far from being able to do the most basic things for ourselves anymore—and here you can make your own clothes."

"I can make anything that's made of fabric," I said, enjoying the rare praise. Not many people truly appreciated the skills of a seamstress.

"But you make most of your money hemming pants for people?"

"It's easy. Takes me maybe ten minutes, start to finish, and I charge them eight dollars for it."

He started taking out the stuff for dinner. He'd said in his e-mail invitation that he wanted to cook for me, and that if upon meeting I thought he was a freak and didn't want to stay, I could leave at any point. He'd followed the statement with a smiley-face emoticon.

I wondered what a computer engineer with gold-painted toes would cook for dinner.

"You should be making your own line of clothes, that's what you should be doing."

"I don't think it's that easy," I said.

"Start small. Make some dresses like you're wearing, for those frou-frou shops down in the Pearl District, or some of the funky ones on Broadway."

"I'm sure they have their own lines they like to buy."

"Can't hurt to try."

"Maybe." And maybe I could like someone who saw a seamstress as a talented person with a lot of potential. Maybe I could get used to the toenails. At least they weren't pink.

Sassy came into the kitchen, followed closely by a gray and white cat, whose name I couldn't remember. "Here, kitty, kitties," Tyler said, bending to pet his cats. "Whatcha been up to? Kitty kitties," he cooed, as they arched under his hands, enjoying the attention. Little bits of cat fur and dander floated in the air.

"You had them long?" I asked.

"Since they were kittens. They're my buddies. You like cats?"

"They're all right. I'm more of a dog person, I think. Growing up, we always had both."

He brought cheap plates and silverware over to the chrome-and-fiberglass table. "Sorry about the lack of china. The kitchen is way down on my list."

"That's all right." Maybe I could be the one to choose how to redo it, traditional female task though it sounded. I arranged the silverware on the table as he went back for the salad and dressing, and a cutting board with a loaf of bread.

"First course," he said, sitting.

I looked in the salad bowl for tongs or oversize forks, and there were none. "Uh..." I said, making salad-grasping gestures with my hands.

"Damn, that's right." He reached into the bowl and took a double handful of the salad, then paused, lettuce and greens mid-flight. "You don't mind, do you?"

"Uh...no," I said, thinking of those two cats that he'd just been petting.

"Inelegant, I know. Sorry about that." He dumped the salad on my plate.

"Thanks." I peered at it for cat hair, trying to not wrinkle my nose and wondering if I could put a single leaf in my mouth without retching. "Is that kale?" I asked, spotting the leathery green.

"Yeah."

"I didn't know anyone actually ate kale. I thought it was just used as decoration on salad bars." Oh, bad Hannah.

"It's got lots of beta-carotene."

I smiled and doused my salad with the oil and vinegar dressing. Maybe it would neutralize the cat dander. The bread looked as if it had about forty different grains and seeds. The main course was in a Crock-Pot: some sort of Spanish-style ratatouille.

"You aren't a vegetarian, right?" I asked. He'd claimed not to be, via e-mail.

"No, I'll eat any animal I could kill myself."

"Like what?"

"Fish, eggs," he said. "And of course I eat dairy. You've got to have ice cream." He smiled winningly.

"That's it?"

"If I was really hungry, maybe a chicken," he conceded.

"Have you ever killed a fish or a chicken, personally?"

"When I was a kid, I went fishing and caught a few things. Never a chicken, though."

"When I was little I went fishing with my dad," I

said. "We caught a trout, but Dad had misplaced the club, so he beat it to death with a coffee mug."

"God, that's awful."

"It left a certain impression on my mind. Still, if I were really hungry, I don't think I'd have trouble taking down a cow."

He grimaced. "But you couldn't eat all that."

"Sure I could. Eventually. Or I'd chop it up and feed it to my friends and family."

He shook his head. "Beef consumption is destroying the earth."

"All the more reason to kill one."

He laughed, as if he wasn't sure whether or not I was joking. I myself wasn't sure why I was suddenly making an effort to be unpleasant. Yes, the man wore toenail polish, and yes he had served me dander-infested kale, but that hardly seemed reason enough to send out those "don't get close to me" signals.

There was nothing that was truly wrong with the guy, no major red flags, so what was my problem? No one was going to be exactly like me, and any guy was going to have quirks that were annoying. Tyler seemed basically nice, and like a responsible man.

I really should try harder to like him.

"Do you ever nude sunbathe?" he asked.

"What? No!"

"Never? You should try it."

"Do *you?*" I asked.

"At Sauvie's Island, sure."

"No, I just couldn't see myself doing that," I said.

"Too shy? There's nothing sexual about it. Whole families go out there."

"Too shy, but also it's just not me. That's..." I waved my hand around, trying to find the words, "that's just not a Hannah O'Dowd activity." It's a fake-o-Bohemian-kale-eater activity, is what it was. "I think I like to stay a little further within the social norms, much as I hate to admit it."

"Hey, that's cool. It's good to step out of the comfort zone once in a while, but I can understand a need for boundaries."

"Where'd you get the bread?" I asked, picking up a heavy slice and smearing it with butter. It looked like bird food.

"A bakery on Broadway."

I bit into the bread, and two chews later bit down on something hard, something that jarred my jaw and shot pain into a tooth on my right side.

I whimpered, and worked the mushed bread around my mouth with my tongue, looking for the offending item, but there were so many seeds and grains I couldn't tell which it had been. And then I found something ragged, and spit it into my palm.

It looked like a piece of metal. I spit the rest of the bread into my hand and dumped it on my salad plate, and that's when my tongue found it.

The hole. In my tooth. It had been part of a filling I'd spit out.

I whimpered again.

"Hannah?"

A flush of panicked heat washed over me, and I felt sweat break out. Fear and horror ran in waves over my body, as my tongue retreated, then touched lightly again upon the gaping maw at the top and side of one of my lower molars. It wasn't even the cold-sensitive tooth, or the one that felt weird after I clenched my jaw for too long. It was a different tooth entirely.

Oh, God. My tooth. I had a huge hole in my tooth. I felt sick.

"Hannah, what is it?"

"My filling," I said. "My filling fell out. Oh, God. What am I going to do?"

"It's Saturday. I wonder if any dentists are open?" I whined.

"Does it hurt? Can you wait until Monday, do you think?"

"You don't understand! My tooth!" I shoved back from the table and ran to the bathroom, and then was afraid to look in the mirror. I started to open my mouth, but I didn't want to see it. I didn't want to know how bad it was. It didn't hurt, but the hole, the ragged hole, oh, God!

I was trembling and sweating, the heat of panic still washing over me in waves.

"Hannah, get a grip," Tyler said, standing in the bathroom doorway. "People lose fillings all the time. It's not that big a deal."

"You aren't the one with the crater in your mouth!" I said.

"You can't do anything about it now, so just chill."

"Your stupid fifty-grain bread did this. Who eats food like that? And kale?" If he weren't a vegetarian rodent in nail polish, this wouldn't have happened. My tooth would still be whole. I hated him, and his stupid vegetarian food.

"Hey, that's good bread. It's six bucks a loaf."

"Well excuse me for wasting twenty-five cents' worth, breaking my tooth," I said, on the verge of tears. I pushed past him and lurched back to the kitchen, where I'd left my purse. I dug out my cell phone.

"What are you doing?" he asked, following me. "You can use my phone if you need to make a call. I have an emergency number for the dental clinic I go to. Do you want it?"

I ignored him, and dialed. *Be there, be there. Please be there.*

"Hello?" Scott answered.

"Scott! My tooth, I broke my tooth, this big chunk of metal fell out and now half my tooth is gone."

"Hannah?"

"My tooth!"

"Hannah, it's okay. It's okay, whatever it is, I can fix it."

"It's going to hurt," I said. "Are you going to have to pull what's left? Do a root canal?"

"Hannah, it probably feels a lot worse to your tongue than it actually is. I deal with this all the time. You're going to be fine. And nothing is going to hurt, I promise you."

"When?" I asked.

"There's probably no hurry. I can look at it right now, if you want, and then we can take care of it on Monday."

"I can't go all night like this," I said, turning toward the kitchen wall for privacy, my voice almost a whisper.

He was silent a moment, and then, "Okay. Meet me in front of my office building."

"Fifteen minutes, I'll be there," I said.

"Don't get in a wreck on the way. Or do you want me to pick you up?"

"No, I'll meet you. It's faster."

"Okay."

"Thank you, Scott. Thank you. Thank you so much."

"Yeah, well, you'll owe me dinner."

We said goodbye and I hung up. I turned to Tyler. "I've got to go," I said.

"Hey, look, I'm sorry you broke your filling and all."

I couldn't concentrate on him. Tyler, who was Tyler? Nothing mattered but my tooth, my gaping-holed tooth. I got my purse and took out my car keys, heading for the door. "Sorry, I have to go," I said in his general direction.

"Was that a dentist you were talking to?"

I nodded, still walking.

"That's good luck, having a friend like that," he said.

"Yes."

He got ahead of me and opened the door, then walked me to my car. "So, you know, before the bread thing I thought things were going pretty well. Can I call you, you know, after you get your tooth fixed?"

I paused at my open car door, ready to get in. "I can't think about that right now." What was he talking about? Another date?

"Oh, okay, I understand. You look pretty shaken up. Call me."

I stared at him a moment longer, this stranger with an earring—why would I call him?—then shook myself and got in the car.

My tooth...

* * *

"You're shivering," Scott said.

"I know," I said, my muscles jittering. "I've got to use the ladies' room." I held my stomach and dashed across the semidark waiting room and around the corner to where I knew the rest room to be. I'd been to his office before, but never for more than a few minutes, and never as a patient.

I locked the door behind me and went to sit on the toilet, still shivering, my bowels feeling ready to let go. But nothing came. I sat there, shaking, bent forward with my face and arms resting on my knees, until Scott knocked.

"Hannah? You okay in there?"

"Yes." I got up and flushed, and ran water in the sink, letting it rush over my fingertips, postponing the opening of the door.

"You don't look so good," he said when I came out.

"I don't feel so good."

He frowned. "You're afraid, aren't you? I mean, really afraid."

I nodded. "I know it doesn't make sense. I know you can give me novocaine and I probably won't feel too much, but I can't help it."

"What is it that you're afraid of?"

"I don't know. I really don't," I said.

"If this is just a bit of broken off tooth or filling, I promise you, it's not going to be hard to fix. I'll either patch it, or if enough is missing, put on a crown."

"Will you have to drill?" I asked.

"I don't know yet. I might not. But if I do, I'll get out the lidocaine and numb you up until you drool, I promise."

"Lidocaine?"

"No one uses novocaine anymore."

He opened a hall cupboard and took out a synthetic blanket, the type they have in airplanes. He shook it out and handed it to me.

"Thanks," I said, and wrapped it around my shoulders.

"You want to see my toy drawer?"

"Is that some kind of come-on?"

He laughed. "Not hardly. You don't think I want a lawsuit on my hands, for inappropriate behavior with a patient, do you? No, these are real toys."

He led me to a large drawer low in the hall wall, and motioned for me to open it. I did, and inside found several dozen cheap toys, from plastic dinosaurs to super balls to fake jewelry.

"These are for the kids?"

"It gives them something to look forward to—choosing one at the end of the visit. Positive reinforcement for the dentist experience, you know. They also get a toothbrush and floss, of course."

I picked out a pseudo-pearl bracelet and modeled it on my wrist. "Affordable, yet elegant."

"But you don't get it yet. Put it back, or I'll tell your mother."

"Ooo! Dire threat!" I smiled up at him, and shut the drawer, bracelet inside. My shivering had lessened.

"And this is Elizabeth," he said, leading me to a bird cage that had been converted into a lion's den. He opened the wire door and lifted out a stuffed baby-blue lion with a silky white mane. "Elizabeth is going to come with you to the big chair, and sit in your lap."

I took the lion in the hand that wasn't holding the blanket closed around me. "She's very soft."

"And clean. She gets regular baths in the washer."

"Poor Elizabeth."

"She's a dedicated professional. She can handle it. Actually, most of the time she stays in the cage. I discovered pretty quickly that while she might help keep kids quiet in the chair, they throw a screaming fit when I try to take her back. She's only for the hardcore cases."

"Does she usually work for frightened adults, as well?"

"I don't offer her to them."

"Too bad." I would have been too embarrassed to carry a stuffed animal around his office during the day, with witnesses, but right now I was glad to have the lion. It was at once both soothing and ludicrous, and above all distracting.

I followed him to the exam area, with its padded reclining chair and the light on the overhead arm. The familiar smells of dentist office reached down deep inside me and set off a fresh bout of shivering. I kneaded Elizabeth and sat sideways on the chair, staring at the poster of a panda on the wall while Scott fussed around.

He turned back to me, wearing latex gloves. "First things first. Let me take a look at this immense crater that's ruined your life."

I couldn't seem to speak, so I scooted fully into the chair and leaned back, letting myself recline as Scott worked the controls. I shut my eyes and concentrated on the soft feel of Elizabeth and the blanket in my hands, trying to pretend I was somewhere else.

"It's going to be okay, Hannah. I promise," he said.

I nodded and opened my mouth, but I didn't believe him.

He clicked on the overhead light, and then I felt the touch of his gloved fingers on my chin, turning my head, and on the edge of my lips. I caught the touch of the cool metal mirror next, and then the testing probes of one of those awful tools that figured so prominently in my dental fears. My jaw moved with the pressure of his poking, and I shut my eyes even tighter, trying to hold still, and trying not to whimper.

"We'll do an X ray to be sure, but I think it's good news," he said, withdrawing.

I opened my eyes. "No root canal?"

He smiled, looking at ease. It was the relaxed attitude that reassured me, more than whatever he was about to say possibly could. "This'll be a piece of cake. You probably won't even need the lidocaine."

"You sure?"

"It's just a dab of patching—the missing bit looks like a tiny chip, nothing more. The worst you'll feel is pressure."

"Laughing gas, then? Can I have that?"

"If you want it. In a very few people, it tenses them up instead of relaxing them."

"I need *something*," I said.

"How about music, and my own witty conversation?"

"Plus the gas."

"Okay. Let me get you a medical history form to fill out, then we'll go take a picture of that tooth." He turned on the radio, the volume set comfortably low to a classic rock station, and went to get the form.

I shut my eyes, and tried to pretend I was somewhere else. *The Lion Sleeps Tonight* came on the radio, and I smiled, Elizabeth in my hands. Now *there* was synchronicity for you. And then I realized I wasn't shaking anymore.

Fancy that. I must actually trust Scott not to hurt me.

Twenty-Eight

White Silk for Another Day

Voodoo Wade and Voodoo Pete turned in slow, silent circles on their invisible filament, awaiting further rubber band abuse. I'd considered adding a Voodoo Tyler, if only for the joy of reproducing the toenails, but couldn't muster the effort for so short an acquaintance, and one that had really done nothing wrong.

He'd sent an e-mail a couple days after our date, asking how I was, and asking if I'd like to try it again sometime. I'd e-mailed back that I was fine, the tooth had been easily repaired, and that while I thought him to be a wonderful man, I felt we made an unlikely couple.

The truth was that while I might have been able to persuade myself to tolerate the kale and the nude sunbathing, I couldn't imagine where I could fit in Tyler's house. The rooms were empty, but he had left no space in them for another person, and her ideas. Whatever he said about wanting a wife and a family, he was not ready for such an intrusion.

Seeing that in him had made it easier to see it in myself.

Maybe I really wasn't ready for marriage, or was at least ambivalent about it. Cassie might be right, and I hadn't let myself feel for Scott what I probably could because I knew, deep down, that I would fall for him and end up married.

There was still my concern about Louise's prior claim to him, but it wasn't really that big an issue. I may have been using it as an excuse to keep my distance.

I swiveled in my work chair and looked at the wedding dress. I'd gotten it to the point that with another hour's work it would be finished, and then I'd stopped, and not touched it again.

If you sew it, he will come.

Maybe I didn't want him to come, not yet. There wasn't as much of a rush as I'd been telling myself: women gave birth in their early forties now, after all. Maybe I had things to do before I blended my life with another, and before I gave my energies over to having a child.

It was the only explanation for why I would have stopped work upon the dress, or why, for all my ambitions, my mate search had progressed in such fits and starts and with such a remarkable lack of success.

Today I was thirty, and instead of lamenting not achieving the minimum goal of a fiancé, I was instead wondering if such a wish had ever truly been from my heart.

"Hey, Scott, I have a new joke for you," I said.

"New? I doubt it."

We were in the foyer of San Juan's, our Mexican restaurant of choice. Cassie had disappeared into the bathroom, leaving Scott to hold her gift as well as his own, and Louise had yet to arrive.

"So this man has a sore tooth, and he goes in to get it taken care of. The dentist says he's going to have to pull it, and it'll cost ninety dollars. The guy says, 'Ninety dollars, for a few minutes' work?' So the dentist says, 'I can pull it more slowly if you like.'"

"Ha, ha."

"Aw, come on, that's a good one."

"How's your tooth?" he asked.

"Perfect, no problem."

"You still coming in on Tuesday for a full exam and cleaning?"

"Yes," I grumped. He'd persuaded me to do it, and we'd agreed I should see his partner, Neena, just so there wouldn't be any weirdness between us. He'd also promised to give a second opinion on anything Neena suggested, so I needn't worry about having more done on my teeth than absolutely necessary. "Where's my gross-out story?" I asked. "You usually come back at me with one."

"I don't have the heart for it anymore. Dentists aren't really sadists, you know. We don't really want to frighten people. How could we ever get anything done, if they were running away from us all the time?"

"Treat us like wildebeests—hide behind the receptionist's desk with a tranquilizer gun, and when it's the next person's turn, take her out with a dart."

"That'll go over well with the dental board."

Cassie emerged from the rest room, and Louise arrived, carrying a present. Birthdays did have their benefits.

We sat, ate chips and ordered. All three insisted I drink margaritas instead of diet soda, and since Cassie had driven me here I had no reason to refuse.

"So how does it feel to be thirty?" Louise asked. "Are you older? Wiser? Depressed?"

"I'm half drunk, that's what I am."

"You've only had half a margarita," Scott said.

"I'm an easy drunk."

"She's drowning her sorrows," Louise said.

"There are no sorrows. I'm actually quite happy, all considered."

"What about your marriage-by-thirty plan?" Cassie asked, the question full of hidden assessment.

"Maybe I'll change it to married by forty." I shrugged. "It'll happen when it happens."

They all three stared at me.

"Really, I mean it," I said. "I've been wondering why I've been in such a rush—besides for the aging eggs issue—and the only answer I've come to is that I thought that was the only way to make my life fuller. To make it mean more. To make it mean *something*."

"You've decided it's not?" Scott asked.

"It's one path, but not the only one, and maybe not the one I should take right now."

"If you're not going to be hunting down a husband, what are you going to be doing instead?" Scott asked.

I smiled, thinking of the possibilities Tyler had put in my mind, about my own line of dresses. "I'm not sure. I'll figure it out along the way. And, hey, I'm in good company. Look at you three, all still single."

The food arrived, and we dug in with our usual messy enthusiasm, except for Scott, who as always failed to drip fajita juice down his arm. We chatted about work and gossiped about acquaintances, and a second margarita left me muzzy enough to not be utterly horrified when a group of wait staff appeared, deposited a sombrero on my head and started to sing their own version of ''Happy Birthday.''

I was horrified, just not utterly.

And while they were singing, one of them set a chocolate double-layer cake on the table, thirty candles flaming on top.

The song ended to the applause of the nearby tables.

''Make a wish!'' Louise said.

So I did.

I wished for happiness. It was the same wish I'd always made as a child, when blowing dandelion heads or the floating, downy seeds of thistles. Happiness, in whatever form it wished.

I blew out the candles, taking three breaths to do it—to their groans—and then Louise took a large knife out of her purse while Cassie plucked the candles from the frosting.

''I snuck the cake into the kitchen before you arrived, then went out the back door and came around front, so you wouldn't suspect anything,'' Louise said.

''Tricky girl.''

She distributed cake, and then Cassie handed me her gift.

I tore it open with the type of disregard for paper preservation intended to show great pleasure at receiving a gift. It was a deck of tarot cards, and an instruction book.

''So you can tell your own future,'' Cassie said.

"Thank you!" I said. She was always so symbolic in her choices, I had to smile.

I ripped into Louise's gift. It was a hardback book of costume history, full of color illustrations.

"I read part of it," Louise said. "The text is mostly how clothing relates to everyday life, in the period it was worn."

"I'm seeing future Halloween costumes here," I said, flipping through the glossy pages. "Sometimes I wish we still wore clothes like this. Although I don't suppose much of it is machine washable."

And then Scott's present.

"It's not an ultrasonic toothbrush, is it?" I asked, tearing open a corner. "Or one of those electric flossers?"

"No. I did think about getting you the automatic pants press from The Sharper Image, but it cost too much. The digital, talking tire gauge was within my budget, though."

"You better not have."

And he hadn't. It was a freshwater pearl and pale blue crystal necklace, the pearls and beads separated by fine silver chain.

"Oh, Scott, it's lovely!"

"I thought you needed something to go with your pearl bracelet," he said, cheeks coloring.

"Thank you so much!"

I couldn't miss the knowing glance that Cassie and Louise exchanged. I ignored it, and opened the clasp and put on the necklace.

"It suits you," Louise said. "The colors are just right."

I lay my fingers on it, and smiled at Scott.

We finished up our cake and drinks, and then it was time to go. Louise and I stopped in the rest room, and while we were washing our hands I admired the necklace in the mirror.

"You really like it, don't you?" Louise said.

"Yes. You know I don't wear jewelry often, but I like this."

Louise dried her hands, then rested them on her hips. "Hannah, can I ask you something?"

"Sure."

"Do you have no interest in Scott whatsoever?"

I looked at her in surprise, and couldn't find the words in my margarita-bcfuddled mind to answer.

"Because the poor boy has been boring me to tears talking about you, asking my advice on how to woo you—woo you! Can you believe he would use such a term?—and if you want him, I really wish you'd hurry up and let him know so he'd quit bothering me."

"But—" I said.

"But, what?"

"But—wouldn't that trouble you? If we got together?"

"For God's sake! I think you're perfect for each other. I've been trying to push you together for ages."

"I thought—"

"That I'd be jealous, or something? Look, I was never completely in love with Scott, I never thought I'd end up with him, not even when we were still teenagers. He's a great guy—for someone else. And I think that someone is you."

"Oh," I said.

"Yeah, oh. So, please, if you like him, let him know. I spend enough time on the phone at work. I don't need it at home, too."

We left the bathroom, and found Cassie and Scott waiting in front of the restaurant. The night air was pleasantly warm, the sounds of traffic intermittent, snatches of conversation drifting to us from the open patio farther down the building.

"Hannah, would you mind if Scott took you home?" Cassie asked. "I've got to run over to work and pick up my check."

I could smell a setup, but was willing to bet it was one of Cassie's making, not Scott's. "Sure, fine. If it's okay with you?" I asked Scott.

"No problem. We get to take home the leftover cake, don't we?"

"Of course," Louise said.

We said our goodbyes, I thanked Cassie and Louise again, and Scott carried the cake to his car, setting it on the trunk while he opened the passenger door for me.

"Such service!"

"It's your birthday. You're queen for the day," he said.

"You're just being nice so you can get another piece of cake."

"Probably."

He handed me the cake, and went around the car and climbed into the driver's seat. We pulled out into traffic, and started the short drive back to my place.

"I'm going down to Roseburg on Sunday," I said. "Mom and Dad want to take me out to dinner."

"How's your mom doing?"

"She's still improving. She's slow, both in movement and in speech, but when I talk to her I know she's still in there, still the same."

He nodded. "And your dad? How's he holding up?"

"He has...surprised me. Now that he's forced to be competent around the house, he actually is. And he's taking good care of her. It's an awful thing to say, but I almost think it was good for him—good for them both—that this happened. They seem closer than I've ever seen them."

"Nothing ever turns out how we expect, does it?"

"No."

We drove along in silence a few more blocks.

"Scott?"

"Hmm?"

"You want to come down there with me, on Sunday?"

He took his eyes off the road long enough to glance at me.

"I mean, if you want," I said. "You don't have to."

He smiled. "No, I'd like that."

Maybe I wasn't ready for Mr. One-in-a-Million, or maybe I was. Either way, I would find out in time.

And either way, I was going to be all right.